D0391876

The Unknown Quantity

Hermann Broch

The Unknown Quantity

Translated by Willa and Edwin Muir
With an Afterword by Sidney Feshbach

The Marlboro Press
Marlboro, Vermont

Contents

I

1

THE physics lecture-room, with its white-enamelled rows of seats and white-tiled walls, had a hygienic look. On the long stretch of the lecture desk in the well of the amphitheatre stood an array of curiously distorted glass vessels which the laboratory attendant Anton Krispin was just clearing away. He was a small man, indifferently shaved, with a dirty, crumpled black smock hanging loose from his shoulders and a silver watch-chain dangling on his checked waistcoat; when he came to clean the blackboard, which was scribbled all over with mathematical formulæ from the last lecture, he had to get up on tip-toe to do it. There were some students still in their seats, and they watched the blackboards growing clean and glossy under the sweeping strokes of the wet cloth while drops of chalky water trickled down in white runnels; and when the attendant with a final horizontal sweep caught and wiped away from the lower edge of the blackboard the last drops that were still trickling, many of the onlookers felt a pleasant sensation. For instance, Richard Hieck, regarding the damp glossiness of the board, was reminded of the black velvet of the midnight sky.

Richard Hieck pushed his way out from one of the upper seats. Like the attendant, he was wearing a black laboratory smock, which was, however, unbuttoned up to the neck as if it were a soutane, so that his appearance had none of the other's flowing carelessness; he made instead a rather tall and clumsy figure, holding the skirts of his smock carefully about him and yet unable to prevent them from catching in the tip-up seats. In spite of this bulky clumsiness, indeed in direct contradiction to it, the face attached to his rugged skull was of a leanness and sharpness that promised in the course of time, always supposing that its owner led the right kind of life, to develop the ascetic hardness stamped on a certain type of Spanish face. Through the windows of the corridor, which presented the usual between-lecture aspect, the winter sun was shining, heightened in brilliance by the snow on the roofs over the way; under the windows warmth was rising from the radiators; clouds of cigarette smoke hung in the beams of sunlight; strolling footsteps dawdled over the wood-block floor; cigarette ends were tossed into corners; from the open doors of the lecture-rooms stale air puffed out, and there was a reek of dust. Hieck, with his stiff, immobile carriage, his right shoulder always held a little higher than the other, made his way towards Professor Weitprecht's private room. He was going to ask about the thesis for his doctorate.

The door of the small examination-room, which served also as the professor's antechamber, was standing open. The university reference library was housed here; several professors looked down from their frames on the walls; and at the big examination table surrounded by its yellow chairs sat Doctor Kapperbrunn, Weitprecht's mathematical assistant. As a pure mathematician he despised the dabblers in physics. And since Hieck had deserted pure mathematics for physics, he regarded him with especial contempt. He looked up from the tables of calculations at which he was languidly working.

"Hallo, Hieck . . . I say, can you still add?"

"No," said Hieck gravely, "a real mathematician doesn't need to be able to add."

"Splendid," said Kapperbrunn, "but all the same I'd be glad if you tackled this job for me."

"May I have a look at it?" said Hieck courteously.

Kapperbrunn got up. He had a merry face, not at all

scientific-looking; everything about him was rather plump, a good preparation for the portly belly he would have later on and which for the present he was keeping in check by various means.

"A good thing tomorrow's Sunday," he said. "I suppose you don't go in for skiing?"

Hieck, bending over the calculations to which he had at once applied himself, said:

"There's either a mistake here or a miracle."

"Let's hope it's a miracle," remarked Kapperbrunn without interest.

"Such a large minus error as this isn't possible. . . . Professor Weitprecht couldn't have helped noticing it."

"Yes, he did mention it," returned Kapperbrunn, "but after all professors sometimes make a mistake, especially if it's a mistake that fits in with their notions."

Hieck glanced at the door leading into Weitprecht's room.

"No, no, he isn't in there, but I've told him that to his face already . . . anyhow I'm going up to the Klober hut tonight and I shan't be back till Sunday evening."

Hieck said: "If this is correct, it means a revolution in physics."

"There have been so many of these revolutions," said Kapperbrunn.

Weitprecht came in. Over his half-moon glasses he gave the two men a glance that was shy and wavering, and yet there was a kind of watchful intensity in his sharp bird-like face.

"Have you checked it, Doctor Kapperbrunn?"

"The calculations are all in order, Herr Professor."

"Ah . . . well, you see, Doctor Kapperbrunn, I have an idea that this phenomenon will have to be tackled by group-theory methods."

Kapperbrunn pricked up his ears.

"That would have to be well looked into."

"Yes, I'd be glad if you would do it . . ." Weitprecht was making for his own door but paused again.

"It might really have far-reaching consequences, don't you think?"

Kapperbrunn indicated Hieck:

"Here's an old Theory-of-Numbers man—you did publish a paper on the theory of numbers, didn't you, before you fell from grace?—what's your opinion?"

Hieck said:

"I can't foresee all the consequences yet, but I'd very much like to look into it."

"What's your name?" said Weitprecht quickly, adding: "Oh, yes, Herr Hieck, I beg your pardon."

"Herr Professor, I really came to ask if you had gone over my thesis yet," Hieck managed to bring out.

"Your thesis? Your thesis? . . ." Weitprecht ransacked his memory, ". . . oh, yes . . . Kunz has it . . . I expect it's all right, you know . . . but meanwhile, if you would really do some work with Doctor Kapperbrunn on the possible application of group-theory methods to this, it would be a great help to me."

And he vanished from the room.

"There you are," said Kapperbrunn when the door had shut behind Weitprecht, "and I thought this was going to be a cushy job. Well, when I'm a professor, my assistants will have an easier time of it, you can depend on that."

Hieck said slowly:

"But it's an exciting idea . . . perhaps there was no mistake in the observations after all."

"A chief that's always on the go is a pest . . . and exciting ideas are a worse pest. . . . I'll think it over in the Klober hut. . . ."

"I've done nothing but theory of sets this last year," said Hieck.

"Well, you can try it by that method, too."

"You don't really mean that seriously?" asked Hieck.

"In science the absurdest things are suddenly taken seriously." Kapperbrunn had thrust his hands in his trousers pockets and was staring out at the snow. "At least, in any science that isn't pure mathematics. . . . Mathematics is the only science worth calling pure nowadays."

"Yes," said Hieck.

"You know," went on Kapperbrunn, "mathematics is a kind of last desperate stand made by the human spirit. . . . In itself it's not really necessary, but it's a kind of island of decency, and that's why I like it."

Hieck could not think of much to say in answer. Kapperbrunn struck him as cynical. Kapperbrunn was being a traitor to something or other, but it was not easy to say what. Mathematics? For Hieck mathematics was a thrilling pursuit, but he didn't know why it was so thrilling. And then Kapperbrunn was already flying off at a tangent.

"Nobody takes science quite seriously except the women," he was saying, indicating through the open door a few women students who were visible out in the corridor; "nobody but women should be allowed to do science. Anyhow, they used to do all the fieldwork in earlier times. But the men. . . . As for you, Hieck, a big fellow like you should have been felling trees."

Hieck was not the person to skip lightly from one train of thought to another. He could not help reflecting on the primitive task of the lumberman, to saw a log so as to get the greatest number of planks out of it. A maximum problem, he thought, but there's some rule-of-thumb to meet it. Then he heard Kapperbrunn saying:

"Get hold of one of these girls, if you can find a pretty one, and strap skis on your feet for a couple of days. Enjoy yourself while you can, for we all turn respectable far too soon."

"Yes," said Hieck, thinking of the library he was now

bound for. He did not know how to take his leave, and so suddenly made an abrupt and awkward bow like a schoolboy and found himself outside.

2

WITHOUT anybody suspecting the fact, indeed without himself knowing it, Hieck had had a difficult boyhood. It was certainly not because of the humble circumstances in which he had been reared, for there had always been enough to eat, at least until the War. And then he had been lodged with country relatives who were farmers, and he had not come off too badly. No, it was not his circumstances, or, rather, it was his circumstances, for what underlay the inarticulate oppressiveness of his boyhood was some queerly flickering vagueness that emanated from his father, something that infected the whole house and immersed every event in an atmosphere of incomprehensible uncertainty. And even now, seven years after his father's death, that invisible and uncanny flicker still vibrated so strongly that Richard Hieck never quite lost the gruesome feeling which had haunted him as a child; he was still seized every now and then by the same palpitating terror, and particularly when he stood before the door of his parents' house in the Kramerstrasse.

His father had been a quiet, almost a gentle creature, with a full, short dark beard fringing his ascetic face; he had been engaged in some quiet profession that was never divulged and was referred to only as "the office"; but quiet as he was, it was precisely his quietness and the stealthiness with which he slipped away and suddenly appeared again that made the house uncanny. His was an office that could scarcely have had office hours, for sometimes he would come home quite late in the night, and even if one had gone to bed, one did not venture to fall asleep until his footsteps had sounded; and when he came into the bedroom, as he never failed to do, he would gaze at the apparently sleeping children for a long time, for so long that it was almost more than one could bear, or else he would open the window, letting the moonlight flow wide across the beds, and sit down quietly on a chair to remain on watch invisibly. It never happened that he took a walk with his children like other fathers, and when once on a Sunday afternoon the mother suggested it, with a hint of actual longing, because, she said, the world was so lovely in spring, he had laughed right out in a friendly way, he who hardly ever showed a smile, and said: "The world burns inside us, not outside us." And this incident, itself burning on unquenchable and unforgettable, had seared itself for ever on Richard's memory, less because of the words he said, although these had sounded strange enough, than because of the slyly gleeful look that had accompanied them, disowning yet curiously transforming every object on which it fell: it was a disclaimer of whatever existed by the light of day, and the look and the eye were those of a night creature who slept nobody knew when and whom one was always surprised to see sitting down to a meal. Yes, a creature of night who had only strayed into the daylight; and when after supper some time later, on a cloudy moonlight night, he took his eldest son, Richard, by the hand and proceeded to wander out with him to the very place the mother had mentioned, it seemed the most natural thing in the world that he should provide a nocturnal substitute for the daylight walk he had refused to take. Richard had felt no fear although the trees were black along the valley borders and frogs were croaking by the brookside and he was bewildered by the fact that his father suddenly walked on to a mist-wreathed meadow and began to pick flowers. Only when they came back to the town did he begin to feel really uncanny, when his father, who had been carrying the flowers carefully in his hand so that one had to believe they were intended for the house or as a gift to the mother, threw them from the bridge into the river. "Stars in the water," he had said as he threw them in. And it was always like that, nothing had a simple outline, everything wavered into vagueness, and even the mother, who would surely have been drawn by her peasant blood and natural inclinations towards a less tangled existence, had become something of a wraith under the influence of this man, this wraith-like man, beneath whose eye the framework holding things together wavered and dissolved, so that in the end one could no longer tell what on earth was holding the family together, why one should be the son of these parents, the brother of these children, indeed, whether one existed at all. No reference was ever made to the father in the household, and after his death no portrait called him to mind, perhaps because his death was as indefinite as his life had been, an absence that was only one shade more remote, a slight thickening of the cloud, an authentic semblance of dying after the authentic semblance of living, a step farther on a way that had always led through darkness and could know no evening.

This was the queer and shadowed boyhood that Richard had had, and although its effects varied with the various children, there was not one of them who did not carry some of that shadow about. In two of them it appeared as a boundless unrest: Rudolf at twenty-two was in South America and sent no word of himself, while Emilie, a year younger, had literally run away from home after a passionate love affair and was at large in Berlin or somewhere. The second sister, on the other hand, Susanne, who was most like Richard to look at, a heavy girl with a hard face, had been for years preparing herself to enter a convent and allowed nothing to dissuade her from this intention. What Otto, the youngest, would turn into—a child had died between him and Susanne—was not yet obvious; his mother

11

averred that the slim handsome boy was like his father, but his gay and impudent manner had nothing of his father's nocturnal darkness, not even when he put on an exaggerated air of resignation because for lack of money he had been forced to give up the idea of becoming an artist and was apprenticed instead in a commercial art studio.

The general nebulousness of all being, so strongly suggested by their father, would probably have kept the children from entering any profession. And it was a kind of reaction from his father's influence and disposition that made Richard stick so doggedly to his schooling and his studies; in the school with its regular discipline he found at least some portion of that definite certainty of which he had been deprived as a child. And that was probably why he had so early nursed a secret liking for clear and mathematical subjects, a liking which was strengthened during his mathematics class-hours into a substantial vision of himself imparting these delightful certainties to a class of his own in the future. This vision had never faded, and even now he could still see a class of listening boys, among them his own boyish face, looking up at the master's desk where he himself was standing. It had decided the course of his life for him and kept him safe from uncertainty, for he set himself the goal of becoming a teacher of mathematics. From time to time he did some private coaching. And he had already recognized the fact that his impatience made him a bad teacher. But he charged very little for his coaching and so he could always find pupils enough to provide not only pocket-money for himself, but also extra housekeeping funds for his mother. His mother, ever since the death of his father, had been undergoing a slow but perceptible change, a retrogression, so to speak, to her own real self. Difficult as her circumstances had become, she had been growing visibly happier, although she was already past forty-five; indeed, in her contemplative happiness she had grown almost better-looking than she had ever been. And however vexed she might appear at Emilie's mode of living, she was really almost envious of her daughter, who was certainly nearer to her than the other daughter, Susanne, with her convent aspirations. It was impossible to avoid noticing the progressive change in her as she came back to this world and grew inwardly younger; not even Richard, involved as he was in his own problems, could avoid noticing it, although from time to time—and this he even remarked occasionally himself—he turned his eyes away almost with hatred, to evade having to recognize the change in his mother.

3

RICHARD had the results of Professor Weitprecht's experiments spread out in front of him and was trying to deal with
them by group-theory methods. The table lamp was shaded
by a newspaper to shield it from Otto, who was already in
bed. It was the usual evening setting, as familiar to Richard
for years past as the smell of the rooms and the sounds in
them. He knew not only the smell of each separate room at
different hours of the day, not only the precise flower on the
carpet to which the shadow of the mirror-frame reached; he
knew even the sounds made in the flooring when he shifted
his chair, and if he listened intently enough, he could tell
from the vibrations of the furniture and the air whether an
occupant of the room was asleep or only lying still and
pretending to sleep.

The window curtains were not drawn; it was the old,
familiar scene.

In the room the silence was strung to a greater and greater
tension, like a bow. Richard was aware that Otto was lying
awake. They were brothers, yet each was closed in himself,
and each of them had to master alone his task of shaping to
his own personality the innate family heritage. Richard had
some inkling of what this task meant, and he envied Otto:
perhaps things would be easier for the youngster, perhaps he
would not encounter so many difficulties in finding his real
self, since it was not buried under so much clumsy awkwardness as his elder brother's. Yet that was not the only
consideration which made Otto's destiny seem the easier
of the two; in all practical matters, and especially where

14

money came into question, Otto, for all his outward resemblance to his father, proved himself his mother's son, cool
and resolute, always ready to make the best of any situation,
and Richard never ceased to wonder at the boy's success in
adapting himself to his unwelcome practical profession, and
never failed to attribute it to the full-blooded sensuousness
he had inherited through his mother. But because these
reflections disturbed him in his work, he said suddenly in
the silence:

"It's surely time you went to sleep at last."

"That can't be done to order," said Otto.

"If you don't go to sleep, I can't get on with my work."

Otto had sat up in bed. The movement he made was not
visible in the shadowy corner where the bed stood, but
Richard was aware of it.

"Lie down," he said.

"I am lying down," came the answer, a barefaced and
shameless lie, for it was easy to tell where his voice was
coming from.

Richard turned to his work again.

But suddenly lustful thoughts came into his mind. Here
too there was confusion of some kind; here too there was a
lack of certainty. Women were creatures of the night if they
were really women or to be approached as women, for the
female students in the day-lit lecture-rooms could not be
taken as women. Kapperbrunn was right enough in describing them as made for science and also ruined by science. A
few of them were indeed excellent workers. And perhaps
they would do well enough for ski-parties. But a real woman
would have to be night-born, suddenly emerging from the
darkness of the night with closed eyes like the night itself,
so that one could sink oneself in her, lose oneself in her as
in the blackness of the midnight sky.

"Good-night," said the youngster, noisily settling himself
in his bed.

"All right," said Richard, "go to sleep now."

The sensual visions were now displaced by visions of a happier future—supposing that Weitprecht's theory of the quantum-interferences should turn out after all to have rhyme and reason in it, and supposing that it could be properly formulated by group-theory methods, and supposing that this made a starting-point for the general application of group theory to all other physical and natural phenomena, why, then not only would Weitprecht get the Nobel Prize, but the name of Richard Hieck would become one of the most renowned in modern science.

Of course he knew that one got nowhere in science by sitting dreaming. But for the moment his dreams subserved another purpose: for if ever he were in a position of established achievement, if ever he were to command respect—but not in Kapperbrunn's sense of the word—then his life would shed its disguise of clumsy awkwardness, then his real self would shine out through the hateful superfluity of his fleshly body, pure and clear and light like the shining world of mathematics, and he would be freed from broodings over night-women and their idiotic blind faces and would be able to go skiing on sunny slopes with a genuine pretty girl. He did something quite out of keeping with his usual habits—he began to whistle softly.

"You're whistling!" said Otto, climbing out of bed.

"By God, so I am . . ."

Otto had come right up to the table. In his vanity he had refused to put up with the nightshirts of tradition and had persuaded his mother to make him pyjamas. They had not turned out what one would call elegant; the jacket and trousers hung in loose, flapping folds about the boy's slim body, and the trousers, besides, were too short. But the open jacket showed the smooth tanned skin on his breast, and that was the only thing Richard noticed. It was the same smooth ivory skin, the same hairless, bony, boyish breast that his father had had when his dead body was washed and laid out.

"What are you doing there?" asked Otto, quite superfluously.

"You can see for yourself."

"Is it difficult?"

"Yes . . . no."

Otto pulled in the second chair.

"You have it easy, being able to work in the night-time."

"I have to work in the daytime as well."

"Yes, but . . . that's quite different."

Otto wrinkled his brow; he could not express what he felt, it was too difficult. For as a potential artist—or an artist *manqué*—this was the rock on which he split: the unseen forces in the world manifested themselves in the night, it was in the night-time that thought embraced the whole world, but if a man wanted to conquer the world by what he saw through his eyes, he had to depend on the sun. And because he could not express this, because he only felt vaguely that it had something to do with his vision as an artist, he said nothing after all but:

"I'm learning copper-engraving now."

"That's not much use to anybody nowadays." A somewhat cruel comment, so Richard qualified it at once:

"I mean, photography's so much more important nowadays. Isn't that so?"

"We don't use it in our business, certainly, but it's a branch of our work."

And all at once Otto had to burst out laughing, an outburst of irrelevant and really absurd yet mirthful young asininity. He had hoisted himself up on the table and now sat swinging his legs.

Richard was in some way pleasantly affected by this mirth although he failed to join in it.

"Well, what's so funny all of a sudden?"

"Just that you're sitting there doing sums and Susanne's going into a convent; we're a funny family."

And because, after all, that was what Richard thought himself, a warm sympathy rose in him for his brother. Gruffly, paternally, he said, bending over his papers:

"Let me get on with my work."

Otto bent down too, as if to help him, and could they have seen their own faces bending side by side over the table, they would have been struck by the resemblance between the two, both passionate, the one already virile, grave, and inquisitorial, the other soft and glowing with a rather open and almost lascivious warmth.

Richard could not get back to his calculations all at once; something had been released within him and he surrendered to the emotion. But perhaps that was precisely why he found it possible after all to slip back slowly and lightly into his work, and he divined that a group-theory solution was waiting, as if on a hazy far-off horizon, to open out before him. With his forefinger he cautiously touched the boy's naked breast.

"Here, you, get into bed and go to sleep now."

This time Otto obeyed, for he had begun to feel tired. And when the boy's slumbering breathing was audible in the room, the haze began to lift before Richard, and he saw before him a crystalline landscape—no other term could have described it—a shining, starry landscape in which the number groups, although not yet actually distinguishable, could be so easily arranged that, when the whole landscape was filled with their flocking constellations, one could set them all spinning like a merry-go-round and yet in gloriously logical fashion. And although this wheeling formation of the number constellations had not yet clicked into place as the solution of Weitprecht's problem, the vision inside Richard Hieck's ungainly skull with its stubble of hair had accomplished something that was a literal advance into some new-found land of mathematics, an act of creative interpretation; and so there was discovered another portion of that complicated, infinite, and boundless structure of balanced forces which is built up out of nothing but the relations of things to each other and yet constitutes the most wonderful achievement of mathematics.

4

THE Christmas holidays were approaching.

In the corridor Doctor Kapperbrunn was accosted by Krispin, the laboratory attendant, with the dignity proper to a colleague:

"How long is Weitprecht going to lecture today, sir?"

Kapperbrunn twinkled at him.

"What do you think yourself?"

Krispin grinned.

"If it was left to him, we'd be having classes on Christmas Eve. Can't you do something about it, Herr Doktor?"

"I? I'll simply go on strike."

For Weitprecht each holiday was an unpleasant break in the continuity of life. Under pretext of experiments which could not be interrupted he regularly exacted overtime from the laboratory workers, and there had never been a vacation which was not curtailed a day or two by his extra lectures. And ready as he was to be courteous to the point of submissiveness towards anybody who might forward or hinder his work, he failed altogether with Krispin, who regarded him with complete disfavour.

Krispin said:

"It's all very well for you to go on strike, Herr Doktor, but when am I to get things cleaned up?"

He retired in a huff to his room. Even his smock looked sulky on his shoulders.

Kapperbrunn sent an amused look after him. He was on his way to a tutorial class on tensors and, puffing at his short pipe, sauntered slowly along to the small classroom. He liked this part of his duties. He had a natural talent for teaching and he enjoyed displaying it. "Nobody can be a good teacher unless he's just as detached from his subject as are his students," he used to say; "youngsters don't like to see anybody with an obsession, and a student with an obsession of his own wouldn't need a teacher." He posed deliberately as a routine worker in mathematics, but for all his boasting that he was just as good at skiing or tennis as at mathematics, in spite of his affectation of being an all-around man wherever he went, his routine work showed a good deal of genuine although not creative ability, and privately he gave himself no small credit for that.

Two women students were waiting at the door, and Kapperbrunn hailed them jocularly:

"Not off on holiday yet? You're a perverse generation, I must say."

Hilde Wasmuth laughed.

"And then you'd refuse us our class certificates, Herr Doktor."

"Oh, you'd simply send Krispin to get them behind my back. . . . I know the ropes."

Hilde Wasmuth was a trim ash-blonde. Her white smock was always freshly laundered and carefully ironed, and she always wore blouses with a broad bright bow of ribbon flowing out over the lapels of the smock.

Hieck came along the corridor. When he caught sight of Kapperbrunn with the two girls, he stopped some distance away.

It was four o'clock in the afternoon; the sky was heavy with snow-clouds, and it was already getting dark. Krispin appeared and turned on the lights.

Kapperbrunn noticed that Hieck was waiting and turned towards him.

"Hallo, Hieck, what are you doing here? Are you going to start on tensors all over again at your age?"

21

"No, Herr Doktor, but I'd like to have a word with you, either now or later. . . ."

"If it's your group-theory job that's bothering you . . . I looked it up and what I told you is quite true; in Crelle, 1923—half a minute—yes, in Volume I of that year, you'll find a paper on your stuff by Gurwicz."

That was Kapperbrunn's strong point. He had an astoundingly good memory for all the publications of the last twenty years. Hieck felt somewhat disconcerted; nobody likes to have other people encroaching on his private discoveries, and he could have dispensed with Gurwicz's article.

He shook his head.

"Many thanks, Herr Doktor, but it's something else I want to see you about." The two girls were still at the door, and he could not mention his business before them. "Perhaps you could spare me a minute or two later?"

"All right," said Kapperbrunn. "Then you can just endure an hour of tensors first."

He bowed the two women into the lecture-room, and Hieck followed them.

It was a very important matter that he wanted to discuss with Kapperbrunn. At the observatory, so he had heard, there was a vacancy for a scientific worker, and a post of that kind, although poorly paid, would make a big difference to Richard with his precarious income, quite apart from the possibilities of later promotion. But although he had completed the theoretical course in astronomy under Professor Maier, he had not done the practical work, for strangely enough he had never once envisaged such a career. He himself was at a loss to understand this, for now it seemed to him that all his mathematical studies had been inspired by nothing else than astronomy. Had he not always gazed at the stars with his father? Was it not his father who had first showed him the constellations and taught him to love Orion and the warm radiance of Venus? He was almost inclined to think that his life had missed its mark, and it became clear to him—one could well say terribly clear—that it was precisely his father's devotion to the night-sky which had made astronomy a forbidden country. His father's whole devotion had been centred not on his children but on the darkness of night, and his unwholesome influence was still active, suggesting that the ambiguous must not make way for the unambiguous, that the unplumbed depths of the midnight sky and its dark radiance must never be profaned by the light of knowledge.

Meanwhile—happy the man who is capable of being absorbed in something—since he was actually seated at the tutorial table, Richard Hieck forgot his worrying thoughts; without a trace of envy he admired Kapperbrunn's skill in linking this preliminary survey to the general theory of relativity, and in suggesting, from a single example, the whole course of mathematical development from Lorentz to Weyl; he followed Kapperbrunn's lure willingly, and without paying any heed to the lecturer's openly displayed amusement joined in the work so enthusiastically that he sweated, as if he were labouring with the whole of his massive body. And then Hilde Wasmuth, maliciously egged on by Kapperbrunn, started asking pedantic questions which were enough to drive a man mad, and the class became a riot; it was long past five and Krispin had already poked his disapproving head in several times; in fact it was nearly six before the session came to an end.

"You're a mathematical tank, Hieck," said Kapperbrunn, as they made for his private room; "I told you before that you were a born feller of trees."

"Yes, yes . . ." Hieck was confused, and so he burst out: "I want to be the observatory assistant."

And now he was sweating in earnest as he unburdened himself to Kapperbrunn and begged him to use his influence.

"Hm," said Kapperbrunn, "I've heard something about the

post being vacant, but I think we'd better make sure and ask Krispin if the news is reliable." And he actually called in Krispin.

Krispin confirmed the rumour. Herr Sauter (the observatory attendant) had taken a notice of the vacancy a fortnight ago to the principal, but there had been something wrong about the way it was drawn up. It was now ready and lying on Maier's desk (that was how he referred to Professor Maier, the Director of the Observatory). But Maier wasn't likely to do anything about it for a day or two yet.

Kapperbrunn was delighted.

"Well, now we can be sure about it . . . and you want me to speak for you to Maier, my dear fellow?"

Yes, that was what Hieck wanted. For Kapperbrunn, with his manifold academic connexions, was also associated with Maier in some kind of way, and before he was appointed to his present post under Weitprecht, it had even been rumored that he was going to be made lecturer in astronomy.

"Horrid thought," said Kapperbrunn, "for if I tackle him, I'll have to show up at his next evening party. And you've conveniently forgotten that the man has two unmarried daughters."

This argument went quite over Hieck's head. He could only look helpless and uncomprehending.

"Ah, yes, Hieck, that's a higher kind of mathematics you know nothing about. But we'd better rope in Weitprecht as well. All we have to do is to dangle before him the hope that you're on the track of his group-theory illusions. Then he'll go through fire and water for you."

5

THAT Susanne's obsession rose to a higher pitch about Christmas-time was well known to her family, and they were resigned to it. Her room, which she had once shared with her sister and in which Emilie's bed still stood vacant—Susanne herself slept as she always had, on the divan—had long been transformed into something resembling a chapel, and was accepted without comment by the family; but now that the nineteen-hundred-and-twenty-sixth birthday of the Heavenly Bridegroom was approaching, the chapel as usual blossomed into a kind of bridal chamber. Although Emilie's bed was untenanted, most of the holy pictures and images on the walls were concentrated around the corner where it stood, partly because the largest wall-spaces happened to be there, and Susanne now draped each of them in white lace so that one was reminded of bridal veils.

Her mother was the person who showed most understanding for Susanne's goings-on, although she was vexed to think that a daughter of hers, who had grown up properly into a well-built young woman with breasts and hips ripe for motherhood and showed the usual monthly signs of waiting for fulfilment, should yet refuse to fulfil her destiny and insist on sharing her couch with a phantom; since for Frau Katharine Hieck, who had lived long enough with a human phantom, the Church, or the Heavenly Bridegroom, or whatever else one chose to call it, was an utter phantom. All the same, and perhaps just because she had been married to a phantom, she had now developed a capacity for sharing the inner life of her children; so long as the man who had engendered them remained alive, the presence of all this progeny had seemed inexplicable, the fact that she had to share with him the responsibility for their existence had seemed incomprehensible, if not actually phantasmal, but now that his memory was fading, the children had become her very own, as if they had been born of her body without extraneous assistance, and she had a sense of communion with them that she had never known before. In each of her children, much as they differed among themselves, she perceived an offshoot from her own maternal being, and although she recognized that Emilie with her hunger for men had fulfilled certain early desires of her own that were still latent, yet besides this full current of earthly affirmation a small trickling spring in her life flowed, if not exactly heavenwards, at least into regions that bordered on Susanne's country; perhaps it was the very fact that her marital life had faded from her memory that she saw her children as products of some immaculate conception, a mystical process personally experienced, which had traced this frail and barely perceptible connexion between herself and Susanne with her Catholic standpoint.

Susanne, all the same, had nothing of the mystic about her; she knew what every layman knows about the Church; she understood the significance of priestly ordination, the miraculous element in the Eucharist and the Mass; she had an inkling of what the symbols stood for in the services and sacraments of the Church, but she had strictly refused to attribute to these things any mysterious or mystical content, insisting rather on living in an absolutely concrete world where the transformation of the sacramental wine into the blood of Christ was as much a matter of simple causality as the fact that when it rained one got wet.

And strangely enough, unreligious as Richard considered himself, little as he was affected by religious problems, not to speak of Church questions, this translation of symbolic and spiritual values into concrete terms was the common ground on which he and his sister met. For the world of mathematics in which he moved, with all its algebraic symbols, its theoretical interrelation of sets of numbers, its infinitesimal infinitude in small things as in great, found only the crudest expression in the world of concrete fact; and even the delicate constructions of physical science, evolved from intricate and ingenious experiments, even the calculability of these physical phenomena, formed in sum only a small, inadequate, pale reflection of the manifold thought-complexity of mathematics, which was embedded in the concrete visible world as an original principle, far beyond the concrete, spanning the whole universe and yet immanent in the reality of the universe as in its own reality.

Otto, on the other hand, although he was altogether of this world, even more so than his elder brother, had a certain artistic relationship to Susanne. True, with unerring bad taste she had assembled among her holy belongings nearly all the devotional rubbish in existence; even Raphael's Madonna, hanging, of course, above the bed, did not save the situation, for a picture that has been reproduced millions of times is already stamped as a genuine fake. Yet Otto did not make such fine discriminations; he was glad to welcome art in any form, and, rubbish or not, Susanne's chapel was the sole room in the house where decorative values were appreciated. With a professional air he used to discuss with Susanne the artistic lay-out of her room and every year inspected the Christmas ornamentations; it must be admitted, however, that he was always ready to exaggerate her pious indoor decoration to the point of grotesqueness, tying some impossible bow of ribbon on the electric light, for instance, and then bursting out into sudden fits of superior giggling that left Susanne disconcerted and doubtful of the success of her arrangements.

In this way the whole family, beginning with the mother,

made fun of Susanne's doings and yet were not wholly detached from them. Often enough Richard would sit down beside his sister, pick up her prayer-book, and hunt in it for some logical connexion that should correspond to that in his mathematical books, in order to justify the unity of logic in the world. And even if he found no grounds for a logical resemblance, he was inclined to think that his sister's aim was considerably more honest and direct than his own: she at least spoke honestly and openly about the Heavenly Bridegroom for whose sake her whole cult and its apparatus were served and maintained, for whom she was preparing herself, and for whom her bridal bed was decked. Susanne's goal was clear enough! But what about his own? What was he aiming at? He too was ultimately concerned with a shining spouse, a Bride who should mean the whole world to him; but meanwhile this bride was certainly not mathematics, which was merely a pretext although well enough able to enfold the whole world and to reach out even farther than that. He was simply using mathematics as a means to attain something else, something that lay as far beyond mathematics as Christ was beyond the Church which ministered to Him, but he had never got beyond the immediate purposes of mathematics. What was his goal? Where was its certainty, its simplicity?

There they sat, the brother and sister, side by side, two young and yet clumsy-looking creatures, burdened with too much pasty fat on their bodies, breathing strongly and regularly in the body and yet caged in the body, each of them, as in a prison-house. Rudolf was in South America, Emilie in Berlin or goodness knew where, but as for them, sitting there in apparent accord, were they not also outcasts in some far country? For less obviously but in literal truth they too were going their separate, divergent ways, fleeing like the others from the dark night of their father, and like him fleeing again into the night.

Richard glanced at Susanne's eyes and started in horror, for they were exactly like his own—what a look they had!—turned obliquely upwards so that the white eyeball was suddenly exposed, with little red veins running through it, a look that was uncanny and somehow mad. And without any perceptible relevance Richard suddenly observed that Christmas had descended upon the world in white stillness, that there was suddenly a cessation of all noise, a sudden suspension of normality, a standpoint from which the world seemed given over to a warmer, more friendly state of inwardness that was a little mad, a variable point on an unvarying curve. The devil only knew how one was to interpret that.

He asked:

"What are you giving Mother?"

She fished out a cushion-cover which she had embroidered with a burning heart in whose flames sprawled a cross and the long letters I N R I, all surrounded by the motto "God is Love." Blasphemous in intention and hideous in execution, only Richard did not perceive that.

"Pretty," he said. It would be a long time before he could fashion a gift out of his professional material.

Susanne stowed her handiwork away under a pile of similar objects designed for the convent sisters. She was incredibly industrious, for since she had little to bring the convent save her skill and energy, she had to make the most of these. She was a sewing-mistress, a certified kindergarten teacher, and was now studying to become a nurse. She did it all with the professional cheerfulness of those who believe that in their occupations they have already sounded all the possibilities of God's manifold world, the same cheerfulness that for the same reason characterized the religious vocation Susanne had chosen.

In contradistinction to Otto, who opposed an unacknowledged and protean mistrust to this cheerfulness of his sister's because it sprang from a different source than his own, Richard was incapable of distinguishing fine shades in gaiety and envied Susanne hers just as he envied Otto's. He guessed that all gaiety had something to do with one's freedom to transcend one's world, indeed, that nothing else was needed. One could not, however, transcend the world of mathematics, and even though mathematics could account for great tracts of physical phenomena, even though it provided completely new avenues of approach to an understanding of the world's logic, and though the very stars in their courses obeyed its laws, its votaries might be rewarded by the ardent joy of discovering new knowledge but certainly not by gaiety. All of us come into life from lower regions, from the dark night of a mother's body, from the mysterious palpitating darkness of our parents; the dowry we bring with us is night and darkness, and we are all attracted towards brightness and gaiety. Yes, that is so. And that was why Richard was drawn time and again to Susanne, although her gaiety often seemed to him a little idiotic; his was the attitude of one who has been accustomed from childhood to feel protective towards a sister not quite responsible, and yet on the other hand he was looking to be comforted himself; it was a strangely wide compass that bounded their relationship, and yet the concrete forms of its expression were merely those of a petty-bourgeois romanticism, made uneasy by the fact that the room in which it developed opened out into infinity and was blown through by winds from the dark night of the past and the brightness of an unattainable future.

Well, it was Christmas, and since he was on holiday, Richard could employ one of these mornings in making his purchases. It would not be difficult to find Susanne a Christmas present; one had only to walk into some shop that sold devotional objects, and there were several of these round about the cathedral.

It was a blue and silver hour of winter sunshine. The yellow trams whose lines intersected in the square before the cathedral were still crowned with the morning's snow, their windows were ice-encrusted, the passengers sitting inside were like dark shadows, and when the trolley ran along frost-sheathed portions of the overhead wire there was a crackling daylight fireworks display of blue stars. The cold stung one's nose and ears, and like most of the people in the street Richard from time to time created a litle pneumatic vacuum by sniffing upwards in order to check the formation of drops in his nose. A sudden jangling of bells heralded an unexpected and rustic conveyance, a one-horse sleigh, which went gliding past; the wooden shovels of the street-cleaners scraped down the white-cushioned asphalt; and Richard, who had decided to buy a Star of Bethlehem or something of that sort, set his feet down heavily and closely on the hard frozen snow which was strewn with sand. Sometimes he slithered and had to bring himself up with a stiff jerk of the backbone, bringing the blood to his head with a shock. He cast an oblique glance upwards towards the cathedral, his eyeball exposing so much white that it looked a little mad, but he did not notice the snow-outlined tracery of the Gothic building; he saw only the pigeons huddling on the ledges or strutting to and fro. Richard Hieck was feeling more cheerful than usual and thinking of nothing, at least nothing that was concerned with mathematics.

6

ON New Year's Day the family was all at home. Emilie had sent a telegram. From the Riesengebirge. No doubt she was skiing there. With some man or other. Rudolf in South America sent no communication. Perhaps they didn't have any New Year there. Why, it must be summer over there.

Frau Katharine Hieck was looking almost younger than her daughter, who was wearing a high-necked dress not unlike a soutane and whose faded yellowish face seemed to show not the traces of past years but the signature of all the years to come. In the twofold silence of winter and of holiday-time the rows of houses had lost their urban character. It was difficult to be sure where one was. At the beginning of a new year. In this silence, that statement sounded like a postal address. From this day all letters would be postmarked 27, and many of them 1927. Katharine Hieck was over forty-five, but the nape of her neck was that of a young woman, a short, white-cushioned, resilient pillar with a small groove down the middle in which curled small ringlets of hair that were still blond.

Infinitely long the New Year stretched before them. And because there was so little that one could do with this unknown span of time which one must attempt all the same to master in some way or other, Otto said:

"We must drink to the New Year."

They had just eaten a fat roast goose, and so Otto's suggestion was not unreasonable. None the less Richard rejoined:

"I'm against having any alcohol."

Susanne was of the same mind. But Otto persisted:

"You haven't a scrap of the holiday spirit."

No, Susanne and Richard had little appreciation of earthly holiday-making. Whatever was earthly and concrete and visible was for them merely a casual reminder of some monstrous event whose potency they dimly guessed at; they almost hated to see any earthly festival claiming recognition for its own sake. And although they too yearned for human affection and companionship, their night-dark natures fostered their desires into visions of surpassing greatness that were hardly recognizable as human, whether engendered in heaven or hell. Monstrous, immeasurable, stretched before them the New Year they were expected to celebrate.

"Oh, well," said Katharine Hieck in her clear, purling voice, "once in the year one can drink some wine." And she thought of Emilie, who drank wine every day, but while she was getting out the money for Otto so that he could fetch wine from the neighbouring tavern, the thought occurred to her that the boy had sometimes brought girls into the house to introduce them to her. All this suddenly thickened and took shape as the image of a wedding feast where she saw herself sitting beside a new husband. Her healthy blood was stirred and she blushed.

Otto had stretched out his hand. Neither he nor his mother had anything to do with monstrous visions such as haunted the heavy heads and bodies of the other two members of the family. Otto's world was of human dimensions; his desires, his affections, his joys, his festivals, were restricted to the regions of the attainable. And the fact that wine was associated with the New Year belonged to this world of his.

All their various and divergent interests had now concentrated on the wine.

"You simple can't say no to that boy," grumbled Susanne. She had observed her mother's blush and at once felt it as

33

licentious; it seemed to her that she must strengthen her own chastity to counter-balance that.

"That for you," said Otto, making a face. He had pocketed the money and was barging out at the door, leaving the grown-ups behind him in that state of fermenting hostility which so often arises in families that lack a common interest. From this primitive human state Richard rescued them—he rapped two fingers on his bulging forehead, exclaiming:

"He's dished us again, the young scoundrel; there's a new barmaid in the inn and he's hoping to get a word in with her."

The two women looked at each other, and Katharine burst into a fit of merry laughter which finally infected Susanne as well: she, who like her father hardly ever laughed, joined in Katharine's mirth with the sudden, spasmodic cachinnation which had also characterized her father. Why were they laughing? Because the secret and profligate schemes of the boy had been discovered? Or because it was so obviously impossible to succeed in hiding one's private dreams? Did they laugh because at bottom they had no secrets from each other? And Richard, who felt the same sense of release, said with dignity:

"That wasn't meant to be a joke, it's really true."

Katharine said, in her clear, purling voice:

"Yes, yes, but it was so funny the way you said it."

Otto appeared again. He was a little too grandly got up, especially considering the slenderness of the resources from which he had to furnish such elegance. His trousers were of an incredible amplitude, and with them he wore the small dark jacket of his confirmation suit, which had grown too tight for him.

"There's the wine," he said, setting the big carafe, half-filled, on the table.

"Why does a glass jug get hazy in summer and not in winter?" Richard cross-examined him.

"Oh, leave me alone," said Otto, "this is the time for clinking glasses . . . we should wish a wish now."

A New Year's wish! The meteor of the new year was inclining in its slow curve in the firmament, and those who were watching should hang their wishes on it. What an abundance there is of wishes! And the man who has risen from his bed in the morning and put on his shoes, and in the evening after doing many things lays himself down in his bed again, has done much to satisfy his various wishes during the day, although most of them have remained obscure even to himself. And if on catching sight of a meteor he must suddenly utter a wish, it happens often enough that he is struck speechless with horror at the obscurity within him, or perhaps at the indifference within him, which makes him incapable of divining and toasting the wishes of another. In the end Otto found the neutral formula of release.

"Long live Mother!"

And because this was simple enough to wake a warm response even in the most bewildered of human beings, they clinked glasses as if the clear tinkle might prove an echo from their own hearts; they even smiled a little, and actually they were now waiting for something essential to happen, the essential something which made it worth while to rise from one's bed in the morning and begin a new year. But because nothing of the kind happened, Susanne said in a housewifely tone:

"There's more coal needed on the fire."

"Yes," said the mother.

Susanne got up and with the iron crook unlatched the door of the stove; there was still a glow in the burnt-brick cavity and a puff of heat blew out into her face. Bent forward and straddling, her projecting hindquarters presented to the rest of the room, she set up a mighty rattling in the coal-scuttle and with the routine technique of the practiced stoker conveyed a shovelful of coal into the glowing heat so that a shower of sparks crackled up from the coal-dust. She then shut the stove-door with her foot and resumed her seat.

Outside the house, somewhere, life was roaring on its course, grand and full, and each of them wanted to catch hold of it, but they did not know where to take hold and indeed each of them would have snatched at a different point.

"Please God we're all sitting together in as warm a room next year," said Katharine at length in reply to Otto's toast; it was a pleasant moment, since the wish she had expressed included, for once, the whole of the family, although it was not clear whether she was emphasizing the "all" or the "warm." She herself wondered which, and in spite of the fact that the heating problem loomed much the more largely in her life because of her small income and anxieties for the future, she added:

"Perhaps we'll have Emilie and Rudolf with us too."

The harmonious moment, however, soon faded. Susanne's thoughts had already turned towards that evening's Mass and her hopes of celebrating the next New Year from within the convent walls, and Richard's thoughts too were straying, playing with the vision of himself spending the next Christmas vacation on skis, and it penetrated only slowly into his consciousness that some reference was being made to heating, which he felt as a reproach to himself for being so long on his mother's hands. So he growled out:

"Next year I'll be teaching in a school in some small town or other . . . or God knows where else."

"Splendid," said Otto.

Grand and full, life went roaring past. But the struggle for existence was raging in the darkness, the struggle for a place in the sun, and even when Susanne remarked: "Sellinger's have a lot of flannel left from their Christmas stock, and they're selling it off at half-price," the remark was part of the struggle for existence, which is implicit in every sales price.

But since no hopes of a brighter future in the new year could avail to dispel the dreadful tyranny of Time's flight or the fear of advancing age, Katharine Hieck was forced to think of the miraculous love she had yearned for since girlhood, and its possible fulfilment even now, at the eleventh hour, so to speak. And her obsession with this trembling hope made her do something that had rarely happened before in this family; she mentioned their father.

"If only Father had been spared to us," she said.

She said it, and so, like a meteor, there inclined and slowly curved down upon them that image of Death which yet had never left them for a moment. And the guest they were all looking for in so many various guises brought with him in the folds of his garment a breath from the grave.

Katharine could not really remember what her dead husband looked like, but she had never forgotten the life she had conceived and brought forth, and she clung to it. What had she come to? And what was going to become of her? The children sitting round her now were dark and had alien features, and the children who were like herself, with her own blue eyes in their faces, were far, far away. And so she said:

"I have no illusions left."

But Otto said:

"Aren't we to have any coffee today?"

"Very well," said Katharine, "I'll make some coffee for you."

Richard suddenly thought of his group-theory work. And

this abstract and theoretical vision all at once appeared to offer a handhold for snatching at that far-off, ineffable life he had dreamed about. He imbibed the rest of his wine and beneath his waistcoat and his layers of fat he had a pleasant feeling.

II

1

DURING the last months of this winter many things grew clearer to Richard Hieck; it was like a kind of enlightenment, he suddenly knew what he wanted to do. Or he knew some of it at least. Indirectly he was indebted for this to Kapperbrunn.

He was indebted to Kapperbrunn on all sides. Thanks to Kapperbrunn he had secured the vacant post in the observatory. And Kapperbrunn not only took a constant interest in the progress of the group-theory work, but also kept on feeding Weitprecht with hints of its potential value for physics. And so it was really due to Kapperbrunn that the professor, who disliked his official duties and in any case was easily fatigued, instead of letting Hieck's thesis lie around for months according to his usual habit, pulled himself together by an effort and actually speeded up the formalities for its acceptance, so that Hieck might get the doctorate which had now become doubly important in view of his new appointment.

All these external interruptions, however, kept Richard back in his group-theory work, and it was March before he laid the finished results on Kapperbrunn's table.

"An honest job," said Kapperbrunn, after he had kept the papers for two days, "a solid piece of work on a good foundation. We'll get Crelle to publish it."

Otherwise his remarks continued to be cynical:

"In science there are two ways of getting somewhere: either you grow hysterical about it and make wild assumptions, like Weitprecht, or you become a healthy reactionary.

As for me, I've long decided on the latter. I'm always ready to go back to Newton, or even Descartes, if you like, and to throw overboard as hysterical rubbish everything that's been elaborated since." He gave a sly laugh. "Besides, that's as good a way as any of becoming a professor."

Richard knew that Kapperbrunn loved to disconcert people by an exaggerated scepticism. None the less, these remarks filled him with smouldering indignation, an indignation which suddenly flamed into knowledge:

"You don't yourself believe all that, Herr Doktor."

"Well, have you any idea what you yourself believe in?"

"You too"—Richard tried to find the right words; he passed his hand over his head; an awkward smile played round his hard lips—"you too are concerned with reality."

"I don't understand the word." Kapperbrunn was pretending to be stupid.

Richard exerted himself still more. What was his conception of mathematics? A bright network of shining reality spread out infinitely, and one had to feel one's way from knot to knot; yes, it was something like that, a complicated web of cosmic weave, like the world itself, which one had to unravel in order to get hold of reality.

"Mathematics is all mixed up with reality," he said in conclusion, and to Kapperbrunn's amazement his voice vibrated with passion; "the very fact that I can count things is a part of mathematics that is embedded in reality."

"It's a poet you should have been, not a mathematician," commented Kapperbrunn; "well, you've become a star-gazer, anyhow."

That this remark had enfuriated him escaped Richard's attention; on the contrary he was feeling cool and superior. Kapperbrunn was pretending to be stupid and was actually stupider than his pretence. Richard Hieck was now experiencing in relation to Kapperbrunn the feeling he always had towards his mother, the other members of the family, and, in fact, most people he met: an amazement, tempered with hatred, at the volubility of the human race, the infamous readiness with which people strung words together into half-articulate speech without having the slightest inkling of the essential meaning of things, which alone was of any consequence and alone made speech justifiable. The sin of not-knowing, the stupidity of not-wanting-to-know! And perhaps only because at this moment he was so filled with hatred of Kapperbrunn that he could have murdered the man, and because he was naturally inclined to theorize about everything, Richard Hieck suddenly perceived that it was always this blank not-wanting-to-know, and always would be, that provoked men to murder, or at least made them capable of watching unmoved another's death.

But he made a further attempt; he wanted to compel Kapperbrunn's co-operation in his own trains of thought:

"Everything that happens develops according to logical laws . . ."

"Indeed?" said Kapperbrunn, "I've never noticed it."

"There's always a law, whether you call it causality or anything else . . ."

"Causality is one of the latest things to be thrown on the modern rubbish-heap."

"Well, that doesn't matter. . . . If causality has lost its validity, that's only because it comes up against logic. . . . If we had the science of logic properly worked out, we'd have reality in the hollow of our hands."

With gloomy triumph he regarded Kapperbrunn; for the first time he had managed to formulate the vague idea that had so long haunted him. Kapperbrunn nodded. And with the sudden illumination of a man who knows much more than he can express, Richard Hieck concluded:

"But logic and mathematics are identical."

"Yes, yes, the science of logic"—Kapperbrunn paused ironically; his supple mind had tackled logic too and lightly juggled with it, but he was feeling contradictious—"another of these recent inventions."

Richard felt himself dreadfully isolated. What was the use of these classrooms and all that happened in them? It seemed as if what lay outside was essentially more important. Out there the March storms were raging. The winter had been unusually severe, and it was still wintry weather in spite of the calendar's statement that spring had begun. All knowledge is born from the maternal womb of night; all reality in the world arises from it, and all brightness is first conceived in darkness. And Kapperbrunn refused to admit it. Richard cast an oblique glance up to the bookcases on which stood busts of Newton and Gauss. Who had set them there? The State? It was a question he had never yet posed. Evidently his new clear-sightedness was affecting his eye for even small details.

Kapperbrunn, who had produced enough scepticism for one day, reverted to friendliness and asked:

"So you want to go on to the science of logic instead of sticking to astronomy?"

"No . . . " said Hieck, and then in a moment or two: ". . . Yes."

"Hm, you do make precise statements, Hieck."

"Well, the one doesn't exclude the other. . . . My work in the observatory is abominably mechanical."

"Women's work, like everything else we do," said Kapperbrunn, with the stereotyped utterance of a man who has taken up his standpoint once and for all. And that suggested another of his pet topics: "You don't get any Easter vacation in the observatory, do you? Of course not"—he gave Hieck a look of frank commiseration—"the one university department that has no vacations, only a holiday once a year."

"The working assistants don't even get that holiday," supplemented Hieck.

"Ye-es, the stars never stop in their courses. I'd like to

know why. . . . Oh, Hieck, what miserable worms we are; I wish I were pensioned off already."

As usual when Kapperbrunn betrayed his private feelings, Hieck felt uncomfortable. He said:

"I must go to see Weitprecht."

"Do it, then, if you absolutely must. . . . He's in his room, anyway."

Weitprecht received Hieck with his habitual absent-minded politeness; it was easy to see what an effort it cost him to grasp the situation, and that he was racking his memory all the time for the name of his visitor.

"The Herr Professor asked me to come in today."

"Today? . . . Are you sure you're not mistaken?"

With a little prompting he finally arrived at the fact that Hieck's doctorate was in question and that he had wanted to come to some agreement with his fellow-examiner about the final test.

"These everlasting formalities," he lamented, indulging in a little hypocrisy, for he was much too conscientious to ignore any prescribed step. Above the disfiguring glasses rose a forehead that was narrow and almost rectangular at the temples, slightly freckled and framed in untidy fair hair turning grey. His mouth was remarkably feminine and sensitive for a man of his age. Kapperbrunn might be quite right in his malicious assertion that Weitprecht was cruelly hen-pecked at home. Richard Hieck thought of the unlovely little woman who sometimes called for her husband at the university. Many of the students would bow to her, but not Richard; he did not care to see this excerpt from the professor's private life.

"So you're at the observatory now," remarked Weitprecht, proud to be acquitting himself so brilliantly.

"Yes," said Hieck, and since politeness was not his strong point, it took him a moment of reflection to add: "And I am very much obliged to you, Herr Professor, for putting in a word for me. A very pleasant post." He felt quite exhausted by such laborious politeness.

"Glad to do it, glad to do it," smiled Weitprecht, almost forgetting what he was talking about, yet at the same time feeling that this word he had put in had been somehow to his own disadvantage; he began to look anxious: "Then I suppose you won't have any more time for our joint group-theory work?" His smile became cajoling and winning.

Again before Richard rose a vision of scientific knowledge as a network that had to be unravelled one knot at a time. But it had quite lost its beatific aspect. It seemed now to be an irrelevant tangle at which a swarm of blind men were picking insanely. Something of that nature must be what Kapperbrunn meant when he called science an infantile community game for backward children: there was often something in what Kapperbrunn said even if one didn't understand it at the time. Hieck thrust the idea away.

"Of course I mean to go on with it, Herr Professor."

Weitprecht smiled a little vaguely. "Then that will be all right."

2

SUNK in the phantom of his ego Richard Hieck went blundering through the sudden springtime that had burst upon the world. And never in his life had he walked so much out-of-doors. The observatory was situated on a wooded hill, at the foot of which a colony of villas had sprung up. It lay more than a mile beyond the town, but for economy's sake Richard hardly ever used the tram, and in any case when he was on night-duty the tram service was suspended.

His work had little to do with astronomical observations. Nor did he particularly regret that. For if the experimental side of physics had been rather galling to his speculative mind, the adjustment of astronomical apparatus, the manual labour of photography, and all the routine work in that connexion galled him even more. Richard was not given to romancing and had known from the very beginning that astronomy was not much concerned with the glory of the stars, that a student of astronomy, indeed, saw relatively little of the midnight skies. And whether the apparatus one had to set up was a miscroscope or a great refractor made little difference, except that astronomical routine was the less elastic of the two, so that in some respects work in the physics laboratories was to be preferred. Nor did the subject-matter as such make any difference to the investigator, since the infinitely great is not a whit more marvellous than the infinitely small, and yet at the observatory there was somehow an exciting consciousness of dealing with dimensions that were stupendously great, the superhuman dimensions which so strangely impress on the soul of every man the conviction of a divine immortality, time and again overmastering even the scientist whose routine work they are. If it had not been for this consciousness of unimaginable light-years, unimaginable to human faculties and yet fraught with human significance, the whole apparatus of astronomy would simply have bored Richard, and indeed he was often bored by it.

But he loved his journey home beneath the night-sky. The delicate breath of spring hung in the branches of the fir trees, the scent of dust stole up from the carpet of needles underfoot, a cool, lingering scent. The small inn he had to pass, with its tables set out under the trees, was usually closed at this time; only an attic in the roof, where perhaps the waitress was reading or making love, always showed a lighted window. On Sundays of course there was plenty of movement, and people were still sitting at the tables while moths and gnats swarmed round the little lamps that were strung on wires overhead. On one of these Sunday evenings, when the whole wood seemed to be thronged with sweethearts and Richard felt as forlorn as a twelve-year-old, he had sat down at a table, drunk a glass of beer, and watched the loving couples coming with confused looks into the glow of the lamps from the darkness of the wood, and was himself more confused than they. He looked at the young fellows intertwined with the girls as they emerged from the darkness, and compared his own awkward, massive body with theirs, and it seemed impossible to him that a woman should ever throw a loving arm round his clumsy bulk. That was more than he could expect, whatever the fame he might win as a mathematician. But these not unfamiliar thoughts were arrested by the sight of a couple who came into the inn-garden and sat down not far from him, a man twice as massive and broad as himself and a dainty dark-haired slip of a girl. At first he persuaded himself that the fellow must have used money or force to secure the girl, but he could not help seeing soon enough that she doted upon her gigantic partner, and this observation, which ought to have been a comfort to him, heightened his confusion to such a pitch that instead of going home he turned back and climbed up to the observatory again, driven by an irresistible need for fresh air and a wide view. Up there in front of the observatory entrance there was a small garden enclosure with seats facing a clearing that ran for about a hundred metres straight downhill, and with a sigh Richard Hieck let himself down on one of the benches and stared out over the valley. Straight as ruled lines the trees stood to right and left of the grass-grown clearing; like a bright ribbon the footpath wound downhill through the grass, and the valley lay hushed beneath a slight, barely perceptible veil of mist, suffused by the light of the moon, which was still hidden behind the hill but gave light enough to make the blossoming orchards far down the valley look like snow islands floating in a sea of shimmering pearl-grey. Still farther off rose the mountain ridge beyond the plain, with the stars above its peaks like scattered watch-fires, while down in the valley shone the more sparsely sown stars of the dwelling-houses. Straight towards the town rushed the glittering arrow of a train, its rhythmical pounding clearly audible, the whistle with which it greeted the bridge across the river, the muffled roar with which it crossed over, still audible although the train itself was now invisible behind the brow of the wooded hill. But the vast space between the pearl-shimmering valley and the velvety bowl of the sky, the whole of that great vault, was filled with spring, filled to overflowing; with every breath that Richard drew the springtime invaded his body and was exhaled again; mild and broad flowed the stream of life and the stream of stars above and below.

Richard, his feet planted in shoes, his thick, hairy legs encircled by sock-suspenders, sat leaning forward and gazing

49

out into the fluctuating valley where streamed the darkness
in which the stars were dipped. This night from which he
had come, all the nights he had ever experienced, the nights
that preceded his own conscious life, these he now divined
in himself as night flowed into him and filled his lungs,
awakening an angel in him which was not to be discovered
by anatomy but none the less had always been present, the
thwarted, discouraged angel of his childhood which out of
sheer discouragement had grown shy and sentimental. And
Richard, still in great confusion of spirit, began to identify
the various stars, not a very difficult matter for an astronomer, and recapitulated their light-distances as if he were
getting up material for an examination.

He rose from the seat. An embarrassed, somewhat contemptuous, and yet gentle smile played over his yellowed,
ascetic face. It was a good thing Otto could not see him, a
good thing Kapperbrunn could not see him; neither of them
would have understood what he was after, and they would
both have laughed at him. The moon had risen higher and
the grass clearing stretched olive-coloured down the hill as
he stood on its verge; from the valley a warmer breath of air
came stealing and stirred the grasses. Richard turned to go.
He could not help thinking about Hilde Wasmuth. A good
thing she could not see him. In the wood a puff of wind from
time to time rustled the fir needles. Richard had beer in his
belly and the stars over his head, and the angel in his breast
had folded its wings. So he descended slowly, secretively,
and a little heavily to the inn beneath. It was already closed,
the garden deserted among the fir trees, even the huge fellow
and the girl had gone away. Below the fir wood the
villa-gardens began. The first roses were in bloom, gay in the
light of the street lamps. The houses were asleep. At the
tramway terminus leaned a policeman, he too embowered in
spring. And then along the paved road, beside which the
tramway lines ran on their own track, between fields,

clumps of leafy bushes, building lands, past single houses and selling-booths, Richard Hieck tramped on towards the town.

Meanwhile his brother Otto had not been inactive either. Richard's night-duty had proved a gift from the gods to the boy, and as soon as the house was quiet he stole out and betook himself to a café which was not only the headquarters of his own football club "Marathon," but also a dance-resort; every other evening and every Sunday there was dancing in the downstairs rooms. His flapping wide trousers girt by a belt, his waistcoat dispensed with, and his jacket flying open to show the flowing black artist's tie in the soft collars of his shirt, that was how Otto appeared in the dance-rooms, a childish and yet at the same time a dissolute figure. Since watching a lightning caricaturist at work he had made up his mind that he could do as much, and indeed he was actually managing to earn enough pocket-money at it to pay for his escapades. He roved from table to table, offering to do caricatures very cheap, and sometimes they came off and sometimes not; but since he had an eye for the comic and a sense of humour, he made people laugh, even though they often called him a shameless young rascal, while the women were usually indulgent because they were touched by his young impudence and his mild inclination to dissipation. All of which pleased Otto exceedingly, and the only fly in the ointment was the fact that he had to be home before Richard. Fortunately Richard had a fixed time-table.

In the streets of the town, spring was swelling into summer. Among the houses the air stood motionless, a still column of warmth that reached up to the stars.

His head in the lap of a woman whom he scarcely knew, Otto was lying on the hard bench of a seat in the darker portion of the town park. The nearness of the unfamiliar, maternal body excited him, and then his desire suddenly left

51

him, and he took the woman's hands, settled them under his head and, shifting to and fro a little until he was comfortable, lay still, staring up at the stars. He felt wretched, and if any excuse had offered, he would have burst into tears. The woman above him did not venture to stir; she held the fair young head in her hands as if it were some strange gift bestowed on her; she did not even dare to lift it any higher although she would have liked to lay it on her bosom.

"Do you love me?" she asked.

The boy in her lap made no answer.

She asked again, in a lower tone:

"Do you love me?"

"No," he returned, quietly, fixed in a trance-like rigidity that now overmastered her too. But then he turned his face towards her soft bosom, and she clasped him to her and knew that he was shaken by noiseless, heartrending, despairing sobs.

Then he got up and ran home.

By the time he reached home he had nearly forgotten the incident. He was delighted to find that Richard was still out and hastened to crawl into his bed, for the hour was later than usual. When he folded his hands under his cheek, as he usually did in falling asleep, he smelt on them the odour of the unknown woman. This was so exciting that he completely woke up again. Through the open window he could see a section of the night-sky, and the moon sent an oblique prism of white light into the room. Where was Richard tonight? Otto sniffed at the palms of his hands. They were a little sticky; he really ought to have washed them. But then he suddenly fell asleep.

3

THAT the temperature in a given space always tends to equilibrium, that one part of the atmosphere cannot remain at boiling-point while the other is as cold as interstellar space, that the second law of thermodynamics holds true, that the universe will not suddenly explode, that the sun will rise tomorrow, that our flesh will not drop from our bones all of a sudden without any cause, that our brains are still working according to laws that may be termed normal (in so far as we can presume to judge):

all these statements are based on an immense assumption, all these are anything but certain and are merely no more than likely probabilities derived from the law of large numbers;

yet this law is itself only a probable truth, and might at any time be superseded by the operation of a new law,

for in its turn it is only an invention of human brains of whose normality there cannot be any certainty.

That is the state the world is in, and Richard had always known it, but it took him twenty years to find out that physics provided theoretical proof for what he had long since discovered by personal experience. Of course by that time he had forgotten the impressions of his childhood; moreover, the complacent satisfaction with which he established the fact that the world as we see it is deceptive and is liable to change at any moment seemed merely the inevitable consequence of his scientific knowledge and trained perceptions.

This spring, however, his hidden memories began to come to light.

For it was almost as if the increasing light that revealed his future purpose in life were illumining to the same degree the darkness of his past; the more he was aware of the aims which it was to be his life's work to realize, the more clearly he saw that it was his task to include in some calculable mathematical formulation all the phenomena of life because such a complete mathematical knowledge of the world would help him to complete his own life, the more clearly also did he see through a widening window of memory.

He remembered that as a child he had loved the fine jewellers' windows in the centre of town. There had been diamonds twinkling like stars on a background of black velvet. But he could not remember at what period this had happened, for he had rarely been in the middle of the town. Now, however, he took to gazing at these shop-windows.

He remembered that he used to love the smell of the bedroom belonging to Emilie and Susanne. Now he tried to recapture it.

He remembered a nightmare out of which he had awakened screaming for his mother. He had dreamed that he had gone blind, and when the candle did eventually flame up he could not believe it.

He remembered that since then he had been convinced that his father must go blind, because he had the same eyes as himself and Susanne. And all that had to be connected up with the hateful night-life of his father.

But he could not remember what incident it was that had impressed on him the uncertainty of the world, long before he knew about the existence of physics, the incident that had implanted in him such an inextinguishable scepticism. All he knew was that his scepticism differed entirely from Kapperbrunn's, since it did not keep him from seeking knowledge but urged him on into the boundless realms of science. No, he was not like Kapperbrunn, who jestingly entrenched himself in his *ignorabimus*; he was driven on by that same *ignorabimus* to break new ground, deeply perturbed and disquieted by the fluctuating uncertainties he found before him, and always expecting to encounter something surprising that would defeat probability. It could not be denied that the surprises he expected were always of the nature of catastrophes, and this constant guarding against catastrophes was characteristic not only of his scientific research but of his whole life; every person he met, so to speak, might for all he knew prove to be a homicidal maniac; and this feeling of apprehension was never stronger than on his daily journey home to his parents' house, so that whenever he climbed the stairs he even felt doubtful whether he would find the home still existing.

He felt really more in sympathy with Weitprecht than with Kapperbrunn. Although he was not so easily startled, so *farouche* as Weitprecht, he understood that kind of attitude better than Kapperbrunn's assurance, and in especial the professor's almost incalculable faith in miracles struck a kindred chord in himself; this inner sympathy went to such lengths that he even turned it against himself with a kind of gloating malice and prophesied to himself that Weitprecht of course would mess up his doctorate. And he was genuinely amazed when the formalities came to a smooth conclusion and the day of his graduation was at hand.

As was fitting, his mother, Susanne, and Otto were all present at the ceremony; Kapperbrunn too, of course, with his hands in his pockets and a broad and most unceremonial grin on his visage. The sun was hot in the graduation hall. Richard was sweating in his father's tailcoat, which had been brought out of its retirement and made over and yet was still too small and too short. There were several corps-students among the graduates, and so the various corps had sent delegations, who had taken up their places beside the dais in all the glory of their full-dress uniforms complete with duelling-rapiers. The rolling Latin phrases of the dean were rather boring and yet a little reminiscent of the Church, it seemed to Richard, and therefore probably also to the others present. Now I'm a doctor, he thought as the dean handed him his diploma, and he observed that it made no perceptible difference to his perspiring body. He wriggled his toes in his shoes, the stiff front of his shirt was slowly wilting but chafed him none the less, and his collar was throttling him. The newly made doctor cast an oblique glance up at the ceiling: yonder, framed in baroque white stucco, throned the painted figures of Sapientia, Alma Mater, Sagacitas, and Scientia, while Mars and Apollo, amazingly foreshortened, bent the knee and Historia gazed solemnly upon the scene. Beneath the painted ceiling crossed rapiers were now making an arch to let somebody or other advance in triumph.

Richard was reminded of an unspeakably boring and melodramatic opera to which by some chance he had been taken as a child. He had sat in the gallery and stared at the yellow stucco on the roof, while an endless overture was played down below. It might even have been an operetta.

He remembered a tune that a barrel-organ man used to play under the windows at home. Sometimes they were allowed to throw him a coin wrapped in paper. If one met him in the street, it was always exciting to stare at the moonlit landscape painted on the barrel-organ, with a knight gazing up at a castle and playing a lute, and there had been a tin collecting-box fastened to the organ for holding the coins received.

He remembered two gorgeous baroque chamber-pots in his parents' bedroom. They were painted in panels of alternating flower-pieces and pastoral scenes, bordered with golden fillets. The children had had only plain white ones.

He could remember the dull chinking sound of the heavy wooden lid as it was replaced on the chamber-pot when the appropriate ceremony was concluded.

A stir among the audience showed that this ceremony too was nearing its end. Richard, who was still standing on the dais, felt someone seizing his hand, and it was Weitprecht congratulating him, obviously without having the faintest idea whom he was congratulating, for he looked absently over Richard's head as if he were a stranger while the latter stammered laborious thanks.

That was characteristic of Weitprecht, but it was also characteristic of his profession, and Richard thought of Maxwell, who was said to have forgotten his famous equations and discovered them all over again years later. In the complexity of the world, memory goes astray as well as forgetfulness; and in the complexity of knowledge, in the unmanageable welter of facts, it becomes a matter of indifference whence man comes and whither he is going; the past and the future are alike obliterated. In the press of people Richard looked around for his mother, but caught sight of Kapperbrunn instead, who came up to him and with his usual lack of dignity clapped him on the shoulder.

"Well, how do you feel after this second birth, Hieck?"

"Thank you, sir," said the new doctor, wincing, "but excuse me, there's my mother."

Kapperbrunn had not even managed to say "Doctor Hieck," and as for his mother, she looked as if she were not understanding much of what was going on, neither the ceremony nor the jokes of Kapperbrunn, who remained at her side.

Slowly they made their way towards the exit. Among the heads of the people Richard thought for a moment that he had caught a glimpse of Hilde Wasmuth's face. But it was somebody else. Kapperbrunn, however, was pointing in some other direction.

57

"Look, there's Erna Magnus."

It was difficult to make any headway. There was a reek of dusty clothes and of fusty, unaired rooms. A woman with a flushed red face was kissing her newly graduated son, whose appearance, as he stood there in an elegantly cut frock-coat with his corps-cap set askew on his neat fair head, suggested the legal luminary he was likely to become. Richard, however, observed none of this; it was left for Otto to take it all in, for he was in his element in a crowd. Nothing escaped Otto, whose nostrils dilated to inhale the fusty smells and whose eyes watched the women. He envied Richard for being one of the important figures here. The countless moving feet shuffled along the parquet floor and then along the tiles of the vestibule.

Susanne asked, with a slyly gleeful look:

"Are there doctors of theology here too?"

"Don't know, maybe," muttered Richard. He was feeling disappointed. Susanne was wearing her old secretive, idiotic expression. Where was the Bride of Heaven? Was it Scientia up aloft? They moved slowly down the unusually broad marble steps of the stairway. The white stuccoed vault echoed with the noise of human voices and footsteps. If the right vibrations are by chance set a-going, a building may collapse. Like the bridge of Freiburg, which broke down when a regiment marched over it in step. One can forge a doctor's diploma, too. There are chance interventions which defy all statistical probability. If this staircase were to break down, everybody would go hurtling down into an enormous baroque receptacle, a devil's collecting-box, helter-skelter, his mother and himself and Susanne and Kapperbrunn. A phantom chamber-pot. Now he was a doctor. Where did one find reality?

4

RICHARD Hieck certainly had a feeling of secret kinship with Weitprecht's obstinately irregular and fantastic methods of research; he certainly had the same readiness to believe that a logical and rational miracle might occur in science, the miracle towards which all Weitprecht's illogical irrationality was continually striving, but he had also a shrewd, critical mind well able to sum up scientific possibilities, and so in spite of his secret weakness for the professor, which amounted almost to a secret vice, he had begun to share Kapperbrunn's contempt for him, and the professor's odd behaviour did nothing to diminish it.

Since he was now reckoned as one of Weitprecht's closer collaborators, it was only fitting that he should pay an official call on the professor to thank him for his doctorate. Hieck would never have hit upon the idea of his own accord, but Kapperbrunn urged him to it:

"If you had a spark of worldly wisdom, Hieck, you would do your duty and inflict a social call on our old man."

Hieck objected:

"But he never remembers who I am from one day to the next."

"It's only your face he forgets . . . not to mention the rest of you."

On a Sunday morning Richard set out to pay the call, clad once more in his father's tailcoat.

Weitprecht lived in a pleasant, rather remote street. A row of trees was planted along the sidewalk; the houses had narrow front gardens which were never trodden by the foot of man. Richard, marching along by the iron railings, was equipped—because of the tailcoat—with a clumsily rolled umbrella, for the sky was covered with piled-up banks of cloud in every shade of grey. It was hot and sultry. Richard Hieck found the house.

On the brass plate was inscribed: Heinrich Weitprecht, Dr. phil., o.ö. Professor. Hieck rang the bell. The latticed glass door opened and the face of a maid-servant appeared. Richard inquired if the Herr Professor was at home.

The glass door shut. But after a while the girl's face again appeared. What was the gentleman's name? With an effort Richard remembered to give his new title. The girl vanished once more. This time a longer interval elapsed before footsteps again approached the door, but then Richard found himself facing the Frau Professor herself.

"My husband has gone out," she said.

"Doctor Hieck," he repeated his name.

"Yes, my husband will be sorry to have missed you."

Richard hesitated; Kapperbrunn had not prepared him for this eventuality.

"Is it something important?" she asked, observing his embarrassment.

"I—I've just taken my doctor's degree . . ." was all he found to say in answer.

"Oh, you're one of my husband's students," she said in a more friendly voice, and when Richard nodded: "Perhaps you wouldn't mind waiting, he can't be so very long."

"Yes, thank you," said Richard, much relieved.

He was led into a prim sitting-room. A writing-desk stood in it. By contrast with the desk in Weitprecht's room at the university this was in a state of scrupulous tidiness. But it was Weitprecht's desk; Richard recognized the spidery, indecisive handwriting on a sheaf of carefully arranged papers.

"Please take a seat," said Frau Professor Weitprecht, and

with the fluency of one repeating a familiar formula: "Congratulations on your doctorate."

Richard, already seated, with his hat of ceremony and his umbrella in one hand, tucked in his stomach and made a stiff little jerk forward, which was supposed to be an expression of thanks.

"You're going in for an academic career?"

"I'm a scientific extra assistant at the observatory . . . for the present."

"I always warn young people against an academic career."

She had a faded face, anxious, worried eyes, and a somewhat pinched mouth in which the pearly whiteness of false teeth was discernible. But she seemed very elegant to Richard; she was wearing a dress of blue silk.

All at once she sighed: "Oh, yes." And with that she left him alone.

Richard examined the books that stood on the shelves very straight and carefully dusted, and recognized a few which Weitprecht had lent him privately. Then he heard the front door open and immediately afterwards the master of the house walked in.

That Weitprecht should favour him merely with an incomprehending glance over his spectacles was customary and to be expected, but that he should give him only a brief "Good morning, good morning" and then at once repair to the desk and shuffle through the papers on it, that was a new variation. So was his next move—a precipitate rush to the door, where he shouted:

"Grete!" and then again: "Grete!"

Frau Professor Weitprecht came out of the neighbouring room.

"What do you want with the girl, Heinrich; she's busy."

Weitprecht made a helpless gesture towards the desk.

"There are two sheets missing."

Frau Weitprecht went up to the desk.

"And what's this?" she asked sharply, lifting up a paper-weight and holding up two sheets of paper. "They were lying by themselves and so we put the paperweight on them."

Weitprecht looked rather like a culprit, but at the same time his joy at the recovery of his papers lit up his face and an imperceptible, almost boyish smile played round his lips.

"Have you spoken to Doctor Hieck?" Her voice had an undertone of despair in it.

At once he turned with the utmost amiability to his guest, holding out both hands.

"Do excuse me. . . . I'm very glad to see you, what can I do for you?"

He doesn't know who I am, thought Richard, stumbling over his little speech of thanks.

"Yes," said Weitprecht with a friendly smile, "you have your life before you, the whole of life . . . yes . . ." and then he hastily picked up an Academy pamphlet that was lying on his desk: "Have you read this? Bohr's new paper."

No, Richard had not seen it yet.

"Very suggestive, very suggestive," said Weitprecht; "it's all fitting in on every side, all making towards the same end."

He was of course referring to his own researches. Richard could follow him there. But he could not see the connexion. However, he nodded assent.

"We must hurry on with it," said Weitprecht, and then in a lower tone, as if he were noting an unimportant but inevitable drawback that had to be mentioned: "You see, I haven't much more time."

Richard was slow of comprehension where human feelings were concerned. He thought that Weitprecht meant the time until the summer holidays. As if there were sand beneath his feet, he began to scratch on the parquet floor with his umbrella. Weitprecht watched him uneasily, the metal point of the umbrella was sharp; at length he said timidly: "My wife . . ." but stopped there, as Richard looked up and ceased from scratching. The professor's absent-minded and yet pleased smile again lit up his face. "If I had the time I would do some work on the theory of sets. . . . Didn't you tell me you had done that?"

"Yes," said Richard. "I did."

"Carry on with it," said Weitprecht.

Hieck thought that this meant setting him a new task, but Weitprecht, fiddling nervously with the pamphlet, went on for once to talk of something else than his own work:

"Carry on with it before it's too late; we can't confine ourselves any longer to physics, or else we'll never master our material . . ."

Dimly Richard divined how rich and yet deformed was this man's life. He felt no sympathy for him as a man; he despised him, for the first time utterly despised him. Richard was too wrapped up in himself to pay much attention to another, to feel any sympathy for another. He cast an oblique glance at his professor, who was sitting there so friendless, looking for a friend. Strangely enough, he was reminded only of his own father; there had been no one with his father, not even his mother, when he died. In the next room the Frau Professor was bustling about, and he imagined that she would do exactly the same if Weitprecht were dying at his desk.

"Yes," said Weitprecht, "you know what Kapperbrunn says, that mathematics isn't the handmaid but the mistress of physics . . . do you think he's right?"

"But ever so much has been discovered from the experimental side," said Hieck, "almost everything." Although this was really true, it was an acknowledgment that went against his grain, for he had always wanted to master everything from the mathematical side, and he said it only because the tentative groping for personal contact which he felt vaguely in Weitprecht's remarks made him uneasy. He wanted to get back to familiar ground, and so his next words came in a way of themselves:

"The group theory, for instance . . ."

Weitprecht caught him up rightly:

"Oh, yes, are you getting through with that?"

Richard said honestly:

"It's opening out more and more . . . Doctor Kapperbrunn has sent the results of the work I've done so far to Crelle's *Journal*. . . ."

Weitprecht nodded:

"I know . . . yes, I believe you were speaking to me about it . . ." and then with a scared and angry look: "We'll never get to the end of it . . . we'll never manage it."

He looked shrunken and old. He had stayed young too long.

Hieck made his adieux. Weitprecht escorted him to the door. It was raining in thick vertical streams of warm water. Under his heavy cotton umbrella Hieck went home.

5

THE weather remained overcast. The river was carrying as much head of water as it usually did only in early spring. The town pond, the great reservoir of the old Town Mill, was filled to the brim and sent down over the weir a thick smooth sheet of water.

The dark, faintly oily, and almost motionless surface of the mill pond—pitted, when rain fell, like a leaden sieve—was surrounded by water meadows in which thistles and marsh marigolds flourished. At its southern end rose a sloping escarpment about thirty feet high, covered with thick turf so saturated with moisture that its green verged on a metallic blue. The mole-hills in the grass were soft and velvety. Several hazel bushes grew on the slope.

All this region was important in Otto's life. To begin with, his football club had its playing-field above the slope, and then the banks of the mill pond played a traditionally important part in the erotic life of the town, being glorified by the romantic memory of desperate maidens who had fulfilled the standing threat of flinging themselves into the water. Susanne and Emilie might have differed widely enough in other things, but their gloomy interest in the mill pond they shared in common, and they found in Otto an enthusiastic audience for the gruesome tales. And when the pond was dredged in autumn, Emilie never failed to take her small brother by the hand and stroll out there with the thrilling expectation of seeing the arm or leg of some forgotten suicide emerging from the green slime and yellow mud. This habit of visiting the pond with a thrill of expectation had remained with Otto long after Emilie had quitted the town.

On such a primitive but solid basis for fantasy were reared his later and more sensuous dreams, for which the mill pond similarly formed a setting: for instance, there was the rich heiress, who might on occasion change into a rich widow, but in any case was ruthlessly required to take the fatal plunge into the mill pond out of a hopeless passion for the young artist Otto Hieck, leaving behind her a last will and testament which secured the future of that young genius and enabled him to go to Rome to study. It remained undecided, or rather it was left to the mood of the artist to decide, whether this suicide was to take place under cover of darkness or before the eyes of the loved one. The first alternative had the advantage of making possible a later and dramatic discovery of the body when the pond was dredged, but the second gave the noble and courageous young man a chance of flinging himself into the water to attempt a gallant rescue, which might or might not prove successful. Otto always chose his alternatives with care: he might, for instance, with ardent kisses and passionate, lascivious caresses, rouse the drowned victim to open her eyes again, so that she would think she was in heaven and would fling her arms around his neck, and thus there would be fulfilled on the slope of the bank the rites that had been fulfilled there from time immemorial; and yet after so much fatality and gallantry there seemed no way of avoiding a marriage, all the more since the resuscitation of the lady would make it impossible for anyone but her husband to enjoy her fortune, and since even in his imagination Otto shied away from such matrimonial certainties, he usually decided to leave the lady dead, perhaps to lay her out on the grass with the help of the rest of the football team, or to carry her up to the club-house, where the artist's rapid pencil would transfer to his sketching-block the dead maiden's noble features, and nothing would remain but to wait for the reading of the will and the inheritance of her fortune.

True, these visions arose only while Otto was in the house; whenever he swam in the water or played football on the ground above, there was a distinct falling-off in the erotic potentialities of the mill pond.

The dressing-rooms of the football club were built in beneath the primitive stand for spectators. One went in at the nearer end of the stand into a long, wide passage running through the structure like a tunnel, with a roof going up in steps corresponding to the rows of seats above; the dressing-cubicles, the shower-baths, and the restroom lay to the left of this. Through the cracks in the wooden planking one could see in many places the roof of the stand itself.

There had been a practice game for the junior team, and Otto was now standing under the shower. The tepid water flowed over his slim brown body; he was standing with legs widespread, bending backwards and forwards, watching the water-drops gather in a trickling rivulet which fell between his legs on to the lath boarding, beneath which it gathered in a small pool on the brown asphalt before gurgling down the drain. The reek of sweat was being washed away from his body; he laid his cheek on his smooth fresh shoulder and kissed it, looking round immediately to see whether he had been observed. In the cubicles and out in the passage there was plenty of noise. Feet thundered on the plank flooring. Two voices were trying to sing in harmony: "I kiss your hand, Madame."

Walter Ritter of the senior team, who superintended the training of the juniors, came into the shower-room. Stark naked, carrying only his shaving apparatus. He was athletic in build with narrow hips and broad shoulders, his strong legs somewhat bandy in shape, and he was covered all over with hair. His skin stank like a beast's pelt; his football feet were monstrous growths that looked like two independent gnarled gnomes carrying him along. Otto shrank from the thought that his own soft girlish skin could ever become so coarse and rank and leathery; he raised first one knee and then the other to let the water run over his thighs, but really in order to hide his nakedness.

Ritter pulled the cord of the second shower, wetted his shaving-brush, and began to lather himself.

"How long are you going to keep hopping about there, arse-face?" he remarked amiably, puffing out his left cheek for the razor.

Otto bent down and let the water flow over his back.

"Are you coming to the café tonight?" he flung back, by way of asserting his equal standing. Ritter was never known to absent himself from the café; there was always a train of admiring women to run after the famous football star whose picture appeared in all the illustrated magazines. Otto understood their admiration, yet he did not understand it when he thought of Ritter's leathery skin and the decaying teeth in his repulsive mouth. The mouth was a mere coarse slit with narrow brownish lips like old rubber. The short nose above it showed two large black holes. Ritter was now turning his nose up, for he was shaving his upper lip.

Taking his towel from the peg, Otto left the shower-room. Ritter shouted after him:

"You've nothing to lose in hanging round cafés, you lousy boob; the devil himself couldn't make a good team out of the like of you."

Otto dressed himself. His exaggerated plus-fours reached nearly to his ankles. A garish yellow sleeveless pullover with a red border completed his toilet. He looked like a parrot. His long wet hair, slicked smoothly back, clung to his skull. As he went out, he lit himself a cigarette. Karl Wohlfahrt was already waiting for him.

The late June evening hung low and hazy over the meadows. Both boys puffed at cigarettes as they walked across the miry football ground and discussed technical details of the day's play.

"Hell, it's going to rain again," said Karl, indicating a flight of swallows.

Otto threw his cigarette away and inhaled the grey evening air. Mild and moist, it filled his lungs, which were horribly tanned by too much smoking. He resolved never to smoke again. The mild evening made him melancholy, the healthy sentimentality of his mother awoke in him.

"Do you know which is the finest death to die?" he asked.

"Yes, hanging . . . and you know well enough why."

Karl laughed suggestively.

Otto had meant something else, although not so different, after all, only somewhat less murderous, more like a blissful swooning away in an eternal kiss. Probably much the same thing, and so he made no answer.

They crossed the white touch-line and jumped the wooden fence round the playing-field. The ground here was trampled and muddy from the feet of the spectators. Then they came to the slope of the escarpment leading down to the mill pond. They tried to push one another down, and then, starting at a trot, raced to the bottom in long strides.

Karl lit a fresh cigarette; Otto followed his example. Wide and gently undulating, the landscape stretched around them, to the right the grey houses of the town, to the left the valley in which the willows ranked along the river-bed ran out of sight. Otto's eye for the picturesque was undoubtedly the product of a cross between his father's sense of unreality and his mother's obsession with the facts of life, about which she could become quite sentimental. In the west stood a wall of cloud, shimmering like transparent porcelain, ranging from brilliant blue-black to a seductive orange that was reminiscent of drinks in the café bar. For one who had the seeing eye it was a sublime spectacle. Otto had the seeing eye.

69

"The saving-book's made out in my name," said Karl predaciously; "I'd get the money in two shakes if once I had the book."

"Three hundred marks," said Otto.

"Yes, pretty nearly."

Karl was a tall fellow with curly yellow hair crowning a long, rather colourless face. He was the same age as Otto and attended the Polytechnic. He had conceived the idea of a football betting-business, which he wanted to run, along with Otto, if they could manage to raise the necessary capital. He lived with his grandparents in the town, and he had discovered that a savings-bank account existed in his name.

Otto's reality-obsessed sense of unreality was at all times ready to embark on dubious projects. He had no feeling for the distinction between good and evil. When he divined an advantage for himself, any argument served his purpose; he had the knack of making himself at home in any system of morality, let it be Satan's very own, and he did so without being aware of it. The greatest contradictions found house-room in his soul; one could almost aver that he had led a double life from birth, or rather a triple, a quadruple life, which in spite of his sober practical sense had become capable of assimilating itself to real facts of any kind whatsoever, inasmuch as it transmuted every fact into something quite unreal and fantastic.

"Yes," he said, "well, then, I'll just have to sneak three hundred marks, too."

"Hieck," said Karl Wohlfahrt seriously, "I'm not sneaking mine; the money belongs to me."

"It's all the same," said Otto with conviction.

Louise Grubicht came into sight, strolling along by the mill pond.

"Aha," said Karl, "now I see why you had to come

down by this way; what'll you fork out if I make myself scarce?"

Otto smiled wickedly.

"What? I'm supposed to fork out for you . . . ? Just you keep a good eye on that savings-bank book of yours."

It took Karl Wohlfahrt a moment or two to grasp the infamy of this suggestion.

"Swine," he countered.

"Swine yourself," laughed Otto, giving him a dig in the ribs. With one accord they strolled forward to meet Louise, and Karl politely regretted that he had to go straight home. He took his leave like a courteous gentleman, but before departing he managed to plant a well-deserved kick on Otto's anatomy. The boys' coltish behaviour presented a clear and simple image of adult infamy, but they did not know it. They parted in friendship, while Louise stood to one side waiting with equal politeness.

Green, dark, and wide shimmered the surface of the mill pond; green and wide and dark shimmered the evening on whose verge they were walking.

Louise was an assistant in a photographic studio, and she had made Otto's acquaintance professionally. His talent for drawing had impressed her greatly. She was sixteen years old, had brown hair, violet-blue eyes, and for this occasion had reddened her lips.

Otto would have liked to say: My skin isn't leathery and hairy like Ritter's, I'm quite smooth under my shirt.

And Louise would have liked to say: My breasts don't hang down like my employer's and she's always telephoning to men, and the skin in my armpits is pink, not brown and wrinkled like hers.

But Otto said merely: "Have you seen the new Garbo film? . . . It's gorgeous."

And she lied: "Yes . . . a great artist."

71

Neither of them had seen it.

As it grew darker, they held hands. From the laden clouds there came blowing upon them mildly and sweetly the loneliness of all human life, the night out of which they came and into which they were going.

6

TIME and again Richard was upset by the disproportion between striving and achievement. Streams of illumination would flow into his brain and branch through his nerves and veins, making his blood light and his inward eye far-sighted, yet the result of this brilliant display would at best turn out to be some scientific theorem of limited application, something that might be called a phrase of mathematics, scarcely worth the publishing, and often enough a mere solution of some small problem that was a necessary step in a greater whole but trivial in itself. And even if his boldest hopes were to be one day fulfilled, if he succeeded in discovering a new mathematical discipline, like Leibniz with the differential calculus, like Cantor with the theory of sets, if he should succeed in getting on the track of the miracle of dimensionality, in discovering a logic without axioms, what would that amount to? The sum of achievement never came to more than a small and insignificant part of the unconquerable mountain of knowledge, never more than a small part of intuitional experience and the infinite cosmic horizon, a small, bounded part of the eternally boundless. Nature always threw into the processes of production an enormous expenditure of energy that was a million million times greater than the final product.

In the evenings, when he sat at home by the open window, with the dying down of the street traffic all sounds came up with a dreamlike clarity: a man's voice or a woman's laugh or merely the heavy rumble of a motor-lorry over the cobbles or the single hoot of a passing car could stand quite isolated in space, supported by nothing, without human agency, and the note of sound, thus self-centred, became so strong that one could fancy it the very hub of the universe round which wheeled the whole of space. And, marvellously, without really concerning himself with the problem, Richard knew at such moments what the pealing of cathedral bells over towns signified, and what music might mean to men. But he did not want to think about it; he put it off till later. His ascetic face sharpened; the world was too rich, the logic of things had first to be established.

None the less this reservation was not quite honest, and he realized it. For among the earthly sounds which he put away from him in favour of pure speculation, there was none that he put away so decidedly as the laugh of a woman, if that ever floated up through his window. And could he have been completely honest with himself, he would have known that it was always this woman-laughter that he heard sounding in all notes upon the earth, blending with all music and ringing in every peal of bells. Yet little as he was inclined to admit this, he felt it to be sinful, and not only did he regard mathematics as a refuge from sin, he was also convinced that in mathematics no man could achieve anything who did not keep himself sin-free, or as it was usually called, pure. And that was why he was so ready to deny Kapperbrunn any ultimate dignity as a mathematician, for the man was openly addicted to the pleasures of this world; that was why he was always suspecting some swindle or other behind that mathematician's knowledge and talents. Not to mention the students of both sexes in the college, whose behaviour was often far from untainted by sin, as he had plenty of opportunities to observe, and of whom, indeed, many had taken up mathematics without any inner necessity, merely because there were more free scholarships available in the mathematical department. And he could not shake off the thought that Kapperbrunn had taken up mathematics for very similar reasons.

As for the non-mathematical world, his contempt for all of it was complete and immeasurable.

To Susanne, however, he allowed some value. Whenever he was held up in his work, he used to visit his sister in her chapel, despising it and yet nursing a faint, vague hope that he might get something from it, some access of strength or fruitfulness that might—perhaps out of Susanne's store of assurance—flow into him from this most alien region. Susanne's large quietness and assurance—incomprehensible animal vitality within a still more incomprehensible spiritual world—it was contemptible and at the same time mysterious, and even though her talk was often bewildering or simply stupid, there was a good deal more behind it than behind his mother's transparent indifference. For his mother, mathematics was an occupation like every other; Susanne, however, who certainly understood no more of mathematics and was simply waiting for Richard to abandon it and turn to religion—Susanne recognized the seriousness and importance of his labours. And although he smiled at himself for it, he was always tempted anew to discuss his mathematical problems, his scientific aims, with Susanne, who was miles away from such matters; indeed, he was tempted to submit to her and her assurance as if to some unconscious oracle. He never actually did so, and she would never have presumed to be his oracle. Had she ever dared to try, he would probably have shut her up at once. For it was only in the most secret chamber of his soul that his sister stood at the gate of mystery, a constant guardian, her eyes sealed, a figure emerging from night and yet a guardian of mysteries, although her mysteries were far from being his. Forlorn bell vibrating in his soul, incomprehensible source of strength.

But they spoke to each other on an equal footing, belittling much in each other and respecting much.

"No," she said, "the boy can't be left to run about like this, or else he'll come to a bad end."

Richard shrugged his shoulders. "I can't control him . . . but you may be sure that life's easier for him than for us two."

"Mathematics isn't enough to bring anyone up on. . . . There's more than that needed," she said.

"I know," admitted Richard.

The room was dark, but on the wall, in the circle of the lamplight, an embroidered text stood out:

THOU ART MY GOD,
I AM THY SERVANT.

Richard fixed his eyes on that; yes, he too was a servant, but where was the God he served? Ineluctably thralled to service, driven on to harder and harder tasks, drudging for knowledge that he would never entirely comprehend, that was his fate. Susanne and he, did they really live? Were they not leading a phantom life? Were they not striving to die a phantom death? Was it not Otto who really lived? Ah, Otto had an easier time of it.

Out of the night they came, and into the night they were going.

Susanne said:

"Mother could keep a better eye on him, but she's turned so queer of late."

"She's always spoiled him," he said.

"He has no father," said Susanne.

He's lucky in that, was Richard's thought, but he did not utter it. When his father died, his mother had said: "Now you must be a father to the boy." There had been something unpleasant in this command, and at once he had inwardly declined with vehemence to follow it, but yet felt a sense of guilt for not having followed it.

Broad-hipped, broad-bottomed, and broad-bosomed, Susanne sat there. All the women with whom he had ever had anything to do had looked like that, except that they had also broad, bovine faces, while Susanne's was clear-cut and severe. With that face she would have fitted excellently into a mathematics class, better than most of the silly geese who were students and who, simply because they were surrounded by the severe, masculine atmosphere of science, had hardly ever struck him as women. The daimonic light of darkness enveloped Susanne, but at the same time the beam of heavenly light rested on her.

Susanne looked up from the stockings she was darning and rubbed her eyes. "It's getting late."

"He's out again, the young rascal."

"We have all sinned against him," she said stiffly.

"Heavenly Father," Richard cast an oblique glance at the text-hung wall.

"You shouldn't blaspheme," Susanne reproved.

She was obviously preening herself on being a kind of representative of an omnipotent Fatherhood, of that All-Father who is throned in the starry night and is Himself the starry night. It doesn't make sense, thought Richard, and was again aware of that forlorn vibration. Stars in the water. In this little house here we are sitting together. It's nearly a million light-years to the nearest spiral nebula. Otto is a sinner, he's not home yet. Forlorn echo of a voice: Oh, darkness of the womb.

"Last Sunday he came to church with me," said Susanne with some pride.

"He probably went to see a girl there." Richard noted that Kapperbrunn might have made the same remark.

Susanne grew jealous. "He was with me."

She was as determined as himself; they were both gloomy optimists. Kapperbrunn was a cheerful pessimist. That became suddenly clear to Richard: resignation was needed

77

for cheerfulness; the man who was still hoping and striving could not afford to be cheerful; the totality of things was a devilish mix-up. Probably the young rascal, Otto, was resigned, too.

"A devilish mix-up," said Richard, sticking to Kapperbrunn's habits of speech.

"What?" She had the slyly gleeful look which he knew so well and yet resented queerly.

"Next time you go to church together, I'll have to come too."

"I don't try to convert you; you'll come on your own responsibility."

The wickerwork of the chair he was sitting in creaked as it had creaked on so many previous evenings, on so many countless evenings. Over yonder his mother was asleep, as usual, in her loose, crumpled nightgown, sleeping in the bed that had been the scene of his engendering and his birth. Many streams of life had flowed into him since then, and were even now imperceptibly flowing away again. He remembered when Susanne was born, he was then five years old, Rudolf and Emilie were already there, and he could remember the anxiety that had brooded over the house. And then when the cloud had lifted and they had been allowed to see their mother, it was nothing at all, only a new baby sister. And that was Susanne. The mills of God grind slowly, it occurred to him; perhaps the cause of that long-ago anxiety is still waiting to become efficient, perhaps it will still be reckoned against us; and Susanne's piousness almost appeared to him like an attempt to obviate an evil which was already fated and historical.

"One doesn't get rid of sin so simply as that," he said, getting up. "I must go back to my work."

"You surely don't suppose that faith is a simple thing?" she said, bending over her darning-egg again. "God is simple."

God is in all the visible world and yet is beyond it; He is the Church and He is over the Church.

What was Susanne thinking? Between him and her there was the same difference of age as between her and Otto; five years old she had been when Otto came into the world. He was inclined to project his relationship to her upon hers to Otto: the similarity of geometrical figures, he had to think, although he knew that in real life figures were not so simple to compare and much less simple to portray.

"Nothing is simple," he said.

All streams of life flow into the quietness of night, all streams of remembering and forgetting. Cast out upon the earth, man breathes, and his dream rises from the earth into the sky. Does space breathe? Does it expand to the millionth power, does it contract to that infinitesimal point in which space ceases to have any extension and is changed into the vibration of a forlorn note?

Susanne said: "I heard a door shutting . . . I believe that's Otto."

Otto had been the five-year-old Susanne's baby, just as Susanne had been his. So far, there was a resemblance, but none the less it did not satisfy him. Susanne yawned with the same slack indolence he had observed in his mother.

To come back to earth night after night, to hear its vibrant note, the note that swells to fill the whole universe, to an intuition of the whole universe, and yet leaves nothing behind but a small act of knowledge: that was all one could desire. A million light-years, a thousand million light-years, that was a number like any other.

With shy, awkward fingers he touched her shoulder.

"Go to sleep now. You're tired. Good night."

III

1

THE clouds of early summer had suddenly changed to sultry heat. The city parks became lifeless and superfluous; they were no longer living things in a dead sea of stone as they set out to be; they had themselves died. The pine trees round the observatory seemed dried up; the gloss of sap was gone from their needles; sticky resin exuded from their trunks. The needle-strewn floor of the wood was brown and lifeless.

The holidays were approaching. In the college Weitprecht was still far behind with his material; he intended to devote an extra week to it. But nobody was more in need of the break than he; one could see that he looked done up.

Kapperbrunn said:

"It's the heat; he's always knocked up by summer. But it's a vain hope; he'll go on lecturing for all that."

Anton Krispin the attendant had discarded his waistcoat. He wore nothing but his shirt beneath his laboratory smock. The silver watch swung by its chain from a shelf in the laboratory.

As far as his duties at the observatory allowed him Hieck still went on with his work in the university. He meant to keep this up too. He was attending several tutorial classes, undertook pieces of research work now and then and lectured on them. They were mainly concerned with the logistics and the theory of sets. His position was now established; he was counted one of the outstanding men. His contribution to Crelle's *Journal* had appeared, no inconsiderable event, after all, in the little university world.

One day Weitprecht sent for him.

The table was piled with papers. There were also several piles on the chairs. Weitprecht was standing before them, tired and helpless.

"I must put these things in order, Doctor Hieck. . . . God knows what may happen before the end of the holidays, and it would be a pity to have all that material wasted."

"Yes," said Hieck, not knowing where this was leading to, although it was clear that Weitprecht was resolved to appoint someone or other as his executor.

"You're staying here over the holidays, aren't you?" asked Weitprecht.

"Yes," said Hieck.

"You see, Kapperbrunn's going."

They were silent for a while.

Weitprecht began again cautiously:

"My wife insists on our going away . . . the doctor has spoken of heart trouble and special baths . . . my wife is thinking of Nauheim."

Hieck did not know very well what to say to this.

"Oh, yes, and so I wanted to ask you if you could arrange these papers, if you can find the time, of course. . . . You're familiar with my work; it will be an easy matter for you."

Hieck gazed somewhat hopelessly at the piles of papers.

Weitprecht said reassuringly:

"They're all marked chronologically. The ones concerning the wave theory all have a W on the right-hand corner, too. And the ones concerning the quantum theory have a Qu . . . look here, it's quite simple . . . all the others are marked in the same way, the only thing is that one has sometimes to keep an eye on the inner connexion between them . . . it's quite simple."

Hieck could smell the ancient dust lying on the papers; he had a longing to blow his nose, but he merely scratched his chin.

"The corresponding mathematical material is in that cabinet," said Weitprecht, as an afterthought, and he pointed shyly to the open compartments of a cabinet.

"Yes," said Richard.

"And now I come to think of it"—Weitprecht's face became still more careworn—"that experimental series has still really to be worked out . . . but Fräulein Magnus is doing it, only it would be well to keep an eye on her."

When Richard returned, Kapperbrunn grinned at him:

"Congratulations on your holiday task!"

Hieck felt somewhat desperate.

"Heaven only knows how I'm to do it."

Kapperbrunn comforted him:

"Come, don't take it so badly . . . we'll get a Negro slave to do the work for you."

"What?"

"Why, a Negro slave, or if you would like that better, a pretty Negress, surely you're never thinking of undertaking all that work yourself! You'll find someone among these girls who'll kid herself that it's a great honour, only you mustn't say anything about it to Weitprecht."

In such matters Kapperbrunn was really indispensable. Nevertheless Hieck asked mistrustfully:

"Then why didn't you undertake it yourself?"

"Me? . . . Why, because I'm going away, and because I was thinking of your good too. That's why I put the old man on your track. I wanted to enjoy your look of glad surprise, or else I would have told you beforehand."

Kapperbrunn twinkled at him through his glasses. Now Hieck himself had to laugh.

"Well, which of them would you like, Hieck?"

Hieck snatched at the first name that came into his mind:

"Fräulein Magnus has to finish the experimental series in any case."

"Assuming that Krispin will let her, but he'll be of the perfectly reasonable opinion that the world won't lose anything if that's postponed till autumn."

"All the easier for her to arrange the papers."

Kapperbrunn made a face.

"All that Magnus is thinking of is her doctorate. On the day that she's finished with the experimental series she'll be up and away, you can depend on that—she's a smart girl."

Hieck felt his way:

"And Fräulein Wasmuth?"

"Hm, Hilde Wasmuth . . . if you absolutely insist . . . well, to be honest, I shouldn't take her. Wasmuth is too ambitious for me; she would be so pedantically thorough that, on the one hand, she'd never get through the work and, on the other, she would give herself airs as the talented custodian of these papers, and that would land you in difficulties. However, I'll get a girl for you all right, whether it's Wasmuth or somebody else."

"I'm much obliged to you, Doctor Kapperbrunn."

Strangely enough Hieck was not yet fully in agreement with him.

"Oh, God, oh, God, this heat!" Kapperbrunn wailed. "I'll have to take my tutorial today in bathing-trunks. Are you coming along?"

"No, I must go to the observatory."

The linen blinds were down; the crossbars of the window cast their shadows upon them. Kapperbrunn was right: the heat was stifling.

"I'm going to migrate with my class to the big lecture-room; there's more air in there." Kapperbrunn seemed no longer to be able to think of anything else.

Because of the heat Richard took the tram out to the observatory. He stood beside the driver; the wind rushed past him; the trees of the boulevard flew by. The booths were open; people sat on the shady side of them drinking red and yellow lemonade and beer. At the bathing-place the tram emptied. Richard could see the pool and the cabins; the place swarmed with naked bodies; clear cries came over to him; sometimes he could hear a dull splashing noise when someone sprang from the diving-board.

Richard considered whether he should get off. He would still have time for a swim. In his place Kapperbrunn would have got off as a matter of course. But while he was still thinking, the tram went on, and Richard was glad that the decision was taken out of his hands. He would go for a swim tomorrow. Otto would be over there in the water no doubt. He was free at four o'clock, and could have got there already on his bicycle.

The first car of the empty tram was now swaying perceptibly, and the second one jolted. They overtook a motor-lorry loaded with bales on which the delivery men lay lazily outstretched; they were overtaken by a luxurious car in which sat white sexless figures wearing sun-glasses. Motor-lorries and cars approached them and were past in a moment. The sunny plain stretched away to the mountain line, glazed with heat.

Two yellow tram cars were standing at the terminus. The driver and conductor were sitting on the bench before the little waiting-room and talking in their rough voices. The taxi-drivers had parked their cars in the shady side-street, and were asleep on their seats. In the two garden restaurants preparations were being made for the evening. With closed shutters the villas stood in their gardens; now and then children's voices could be heard in the shadow of the garden trees.

Richard slowly passed the rows of villas. On the sill of a basement window, through which he could see the varnished ends of two beds and sacred images on the wall—

obviously belonging to the housekeeper of the villa—a dachshund was curled up. When it caught sight of Richard, it barked drowsily and gazed after him.

Everywhere life was unambiguous, unambiguous as Kapperbrunn, unambiguous as summers; the tooth of one wheel fitted into the other, the tramways ran according to plan, the dog barked according to plan, the stars revolved according to plan. Drowsily and soundlessly, whirling space revolved around the axis of the world, and a milky white half-moon stood in the milky blue of the heavens.

Myriads and myriads of single lives, myriads and myriads of single things, were assembled around him, a terrifying bathing-pool of things which rose soundless and fell away again; myriads and myriads of lives and things were assembled in his sweating body, myriads and myriads impregnated his thinking and fell away to nothing. Richard put one foot before the other, one shoe before the other, and slowly began the ascent to the observatory, so as to deposit there, according to plan, his thinking body.

2

RICHARD had been mistaken, however. Otto was not swimming in the bathing-pool that afternoon, but in the mill pond at the opposite side of the town. He liked some variation in his bathing arrangements.

Because of the changes in the water level of the mill pond it was impossible to set up a bathing-establishment there, but when the water was high it was a favourite place for free bathing. Since the rainy days of June the water level had sunk by some six feet, and on the flat northern shore one had to wade for a long distance through clay and mud to reach the water; by the steep slope below the football grounds, on the other hand, it was quite deep.

Besides, it was extremely convenient. One undressed in the clubhouse and then ran across the football field. And, accordingly, that is what Karl Wohlfahrt and Otto did this time.

When they were in the water and had got over the first joys of swimming, Otto became bored.

"This place isn't any good."

"How?"

"No girls."

"Mphm . . ."

"If we had motor-bikes we could take a run down the river, Gleuringer way; the girls would be willing enough to come with us then."

"Can you buy a motor-bike?"

The conversation turned to the money they were in need of. Karl had not yet managed to get hold of his savings-bank book, and still less had Otto succeeded in carrying out the robbery he had planned so grandiosely; he had simply not made the slightest move in that direction. They built themselves castles in the air:

"It's only a matter of getting money to start with; then I'll throw up my job and start painting."

"A painter earns nothing."

"Oho! Almost every painter goes about in his own car."

Suddenly he had an uncontrollable hunger for money. And simultaneously something in him imperiously demanded that another should get it for him. He was imperiously and inconsequently seized by the thought that it was Karl who must swindle his mother out of the money. It terrified and allured him at the same time.

"I feel as if I were getting a cramp," he said, laying himself on his back. "I must get out." His face grew white. "If I sink, catch me by the hair."

"Rubbish," said Karl, swimming towards him.

Actually Otto had been very near it, but he just managed to reach the bank. As soon as he felt firm ground beneath his feet, his cramp vanished at once.

"What a thing to happen, ouf!" He scrambled out breathlessly.

Nothing more was said about their money projects. But when they parted, Otto grew chalk-white again and said hoarsely:

"You might come round for me sometimes. What about tomorrow at five?"

He felt just the same as the time he had first gone to a woman, and he could not understand what had come over him. After all nothing had been decided on and nothing had happened. But there was a knowledge within him of something that allured him and strangled him and that he could not name. And although he let no outward sign appear, it seemed to him like the confession of a crime when he informed his mother of the approaching visit.

Frau Hieck was slightly surprised.

"Usually you never mention it when anybody calls for you."

"But I would like you to give him a cup of coffee."

With her arms crossed under her breast Frau Hieck smiled complacently.

"So you're learning to be a home boy at last. Fine!"

Next day Karl appeared in the Kramerstrasse, was introduced and given a cup of coffee in the living-room. The green shutters made the room dark; the air had a cloistered coolness. There was a smell of fruit.

Katharine Hieck sat with the two boys. Her white arms rested on the table. In her clear, purling voice she went through the usual catechism of a petty bourgeoise, asking Karl about his home and school affairs, his parentage and his plans for the future. Karl stared at her white arms.

She addressed him familiarly as *Du*.

"So you go to the Polytechnic? What do you learn there?"

"Lots of mathematics and so on."

"Mathematics? Richard could help you with that." Susanne came in, a dark, nun-like figure, and sat down with them.

"Look, he's much taller than Otto. Stand back to back for a minute."

"Oh, I know, he's a head taller," growled Otto. "There's no need to measure that."

"You're just the same age as Otto?" asked Susanne.

"Really I should treat him as a young man and say *Sie* to him, he's such a big boy," said Katharine.

The youth blushed to the roots of his fair hair.

Otto, who at any other time would certainly not have missed the chance of teasing Karl about it, was silent this time.

The others, too, remained silent, Susanne because she had fallen back into her darkness, Katharine because she felt the boy's eyes resting on her arms and breast and had not enough presence of mind to speak of trifles. So they all stuck their noses into their coffee cups.

Petty-bourgeois bewitchment, but bewitchment nevertheless. And beside Susanne, massive and black, Katharine had a timeless look of this world, ageless as a woman of Rubens, the eternal child-bearer, yet childless, since only her lover could be her child. And after crumbling her cake in her coffee, she crumbled what was left of Karl's cake in his cup too—he was sitting next to her. Then with their spoons they fished out the spongy brown pieces.

Susanne was the first to rise.

"I think the window can be opened now," she said, wiping her mouth.

Light fell in, heat streamed in; on the nape of Katharine's blond neck little beads of sweat were standing. Karl saw them.

"I must go now," he said. "Thank you very much, Frau Hieck."

"Come back again soon," she said, "and if you need help at any time, Richard can help you."

"Shall we go for a swim now?" asked Otto.

"Of course," replied Karl quickly, as if he were glad to get away.

Below they fetched their bicycles, which they had parked in the well of the staircase, and set off, Karl in front, Otto behind. The chains clicked rhythmically and with delicate precision; sometimes the saddles creaked. That was all familiar and pleasant. They glided smoothly and elegantly over the asphalt in silence; in dead silence they bumped over the round-headed cobblestones of the inner town, but in the cathedral square Otto shot ahead and cried: "Which way?"

Karl pointed to the left, where a street led out to the mill pond.

Otto shook his head.

"Let's go to the bathing-pool."

"Why? For the girls?"

"No, but it's muddy out there now, and yesterday I was almost drowned."

"Rubbish, you weren't drowned."

"But I very nearly was, all the same. I'm not going there again."

Finally Karl gave in, and they rode out to the bathing-pool. Again in silence. Except that sometimes Otto made a spurt and drove at full speed into Karl's hind wheel; the two tires bumped softly against each other, both bicycles received a cushioned yet sharp shock, and it became a game which they could not give up although they were both curiously dejected and would have preferred to go their own ways. And so it was only right that just before the last houses of the town Karl should allow Otto to draw level with him and ask: "Are you meeting Louise out there?"

"Perhaps," said Otto.

"Then you don't need me in any case, and I have no money for the bathing-pool."

Without waiting for Otto's objections he turned and rode off in the opposite direction.

Yet only two days later he came again to call for Otto; they had made no arrangement, but all the same Otto was already expecting him. And as if they had come to an agreement, Karl did not ask for Frau Hieck, and Otto said nothing to his mother about the visit. There was no mention of coffee; instead they mounted their bicycles at once and rode out to the bathing-pool. They both felt very happy.

They went on like this for some time, until Frau Katharine by chance happened on them. They were both on the point of slipping out through the door.

"What does this mean?" she called after them. "What are you running away for?"

Otto ran on, Karl stopped. His throat was dry, his knees trembling; he had to stop whether he wanted to or not.

"Good day, Frau Hieck," he stammered at last.

"Why do you both run away like that? You haven't even had your coffee."

"They're waiting for us at the swimming-pool," Karl lied.

"Well, if it's so urgent, away with you, but next time let me know you're here."

"Yes, thanks very much." Karl shot down the stairs, his face burning. They trod on their pedals as if the devil were after them.

But it was no use, the devil was the stronger; on the next free afternoon from school Karl was in the Hiecks' house before Otto came home from his work.

3

THANKS to the forbearance of the attendant Krispin, Fräulein Magnus was able to work out her experimental series to the end. She was consequently busy all during July, and Kapperbrunn had to whip up another slave to do Hieck's cataloguing for him. He found her in the person of Fräulein Ilse Nydhalm, a physics student in her sixth term.

In honour of the holidays Krispin had now discarded his black smock as well, and went about his work in the passages and the lecture-rooms simply in shirt and trousers. The smock hung on the door of the laboratory.

The university buildings were as silent as a telephone booth. When Krispin rustled papers on the third story, it could be heard on the ground floor; sometimes the forlorn *ping* of a glass came from the laboratory, sometimes the crepitation of an electric battery. Richard loved this stillness. It was like the night-time transposed into sunny whiteness. He felt almost sorry that he was not doing Ilse Nydhalm's work himself.

He gave her a few days to get used to the work. When he came then to see how she was getting on, he found her standing in despair before a wilderness of papers which covered both Weitprecht's desk and the table in the middle of the room; she was almost in tears.

"This will take me three years."

"No, no, Fräulein Nydhalm."

She had brown hair, a creamy skin, and grey eyes; she was slim and of medium height. Above her nose there was a little furrow of perplexity.

"If I were simply to tidy them up as Doctor Kapperbrunn suggested, it would be easy enough, but I feel certain that Professor Weitprecht wouldn't be satisfied with that."

Richard felt certain that Weitprecht, who had had to swallow so many disappointments in his life, would have been thankful enough even for a mere tidying-up.

It was swelteringly hot in spite of the lowered yellow linen blinds. Through a chink the sun sent a bright spectrum-like stripe on to the ceiling.

Blinking somewhat short-sightedly, Ilse Nydhalm went on:

"And that would be just a boring routine job; but it needs to be tackled with some understanding from within. I think Doctor Kapperbrunn couldn't have thought it over properly."

That was just like Kapperbrunn; quick to seize and define any task, he would be moved by nothing in the world to take a single step past the first stage in solving it. In this case, of course, even the routine solution would have been more than sufficient, but Richard Hieck was pleased in his very soul that this girl had demands which went beyond Kapperbrunn's conception. So he said:

"Yes, you're right there, Fräulein Nydhalm."

"But how on earth is one to find out where to begin?" She made a hopeless gesture, pointing at the papers.

"Hm, well . . ." His alert brain began to set itself in motion.

Just because in his whole mode of thinking he was the polar opposite of Kapperbrunn, he had never yet brought himself to solve a task for its own sake; indeed, it seemed to him immoral to consider any task except in relation to a systematic whole and to grasp it from that standpoint. And if it was a matter now of putting his organizing and intuitive powers at the service of Weitprecht's *magnum opus*, that would automatically become for him a whole, a unified system to which all problems had to be related before one could proceed to concern oneself with their individual meanings. He had struggled long enough with Weitprecht's theories and consequently had a general scheme of them cut and dried in his head; but now that he was called upon to develop it, for the first time he saw the whole compass of it, in all its insufficiencies and with its ever-recurring flashes of genius. His exposition became a kind of curiously penetrating funeral eulogy on Weitprecht, and Ilse Nydhalm listened more and more intently, her brows drawn delicately together above her eyes, until at last she put on her glasses and began to take notes in shorthand. When he had finished, she said softly and with some embarrassment:

"Yes, that's it, that's certainly it."

Encouraged by her agreement, he immediately proceeded to sketch the main headings and draw up a methodical plan, on which he indicated connecting lines in red and blue pencil.

"There! Now you can get on with it."

She smiled.

"Right enough, I can get on with it now. Thanks very much, Herr Doktor."

The glasses gave her face a look of childish precocity.

"There is nothing to thank me for, Fräulein Nydhalm," he retorted gruffly, and thereupon quickly vanished.

Every morning he appeared at the university. For an hour or so he worked with Fräulein Nydhalm and then betook himself to red-cheeked Fräulein Magnus in the laboratory, in order—much to Fräulein Magnus's annoyance, for she looked upon it as a sort of supervision—to inquire after the latest experimental results. When he arrived at the university, Krispin would salute him and report: "Both ladies on duty, Herr Doktor."

He remained an important personage. And Ilse Nydhalm's attitude towards him showed all the constraint with which one meets an important figure, besides paying him due respect. But he was himself far too constrained to notice this; collaboration was unfamiliar and uncanny to him; and one day when a picture postcard arrived from Kapperbrunn in the mountains with greetings "to you, my dear Hieck, and to your charming collaborator," he hid the card and did not transmit the greetings until several days later.

Ilse Nydhalm was eager to learn and had ideas. Soon she no longer needed his help, and more and more frequently she employed his visits to draw him out on mathematical subjects. It was at once a formal expression of her subordination and a means to cloak her embarrassment. And he gave her long lectures, invariably setting out from the central point of the problem and proceeding until he reached its utmost frontiers, indicating the lines along which research had been working and those it would have to follow to fulfil its self-imposed task. Here too his lectures had the same fault as in his classes: aggressive and authoritarian, he would suffer neither interruption nor objection. For his arguments were arguments with himself, and he sweated as he expounded them, and far more from agitation than from the prevailing heat. Every clarification of a scientific situation was also to him an illumination of his own aims, and the fact that he could achieve and utter such an illumination was like a deliverance from all that lay behind him, like the beginning of a freer atmosphere and the promise of a light. But that he had to put it into words, still more that he had to speak of it to a girl, that the liberating and blissful illumination could reach its consummation only in speech—that was an act of treachery not only to mathematics but also to the essential core of his life. For what he was here discovering—so he was convinced—had nothing to do with the real goal of his life or with that of mathematics, and he strictly refused to let the objective goals of knowledge be confused with subjective emotions. A bright spectrum-band of light played on the ceiling, and his conversations with Ilse Nydhalm formed a strange contrast to the evenings which he passed in Susanne's room. It was a very complicated and quite impenetrable act of treachery that he was committing, and it was leading him back by a highly involved path to the darkness of sin and anarchy! Oh, soundless, forlorn vibration in the universe of space! But any objective observer could not have helped noting that for some time now Richard Hieck had been giving more attention to his personal appearance.

In the mornings he usually went to the bathing-pool.

He always swam six lengths of the pool—a self-imposed decree which he kept strictly—and then climbed out by the slippery cracked wooden steps. Then he sat down on the concrete edge of the pool, letting his feet hang in the water, and contemplated the white rows of bathing-towels, which, gently inflated by the morning breeze, hung like bunting from two wide-stretched clothes-lines on the opposite side. A little further on he could see the avenue, with the trees all bent to the same slant by the western winter storms. The yellow tram cars flew by, swaying and clattering.

The swimming-master Vinzenz Ulreich, bare-armed and muscular in his blue-striped jersey and white linen trousers, was fishing yellowish-green leaves out of the pool with a little net attached to a long pole. The water slapped softly against the concrete walls.

Suddenly Doctor Richard Hieck's name was called. The voice came from the water.

There were only a few bathers there. Streaks of light lay glittering on the water; Richard blinked and could make out nothing. Someone was swimming hand over hand to the steps beside which he was sitting. The figure seated itself on the steps and repeated:

"Good morning, Doctor Hieck."

Seen from above, the low cut of the costume at the bosom

indicated that the figure's sex was feminine. But the head in its white bathing-cap might just as well have been that of a boy.

"Good morning," replied Richard uncertainly.

The stranger made herself known: "Don't rack your brains; it's Erna Magnus." She drew up her legs and clasped her knees. All of her was light brown, a pale coffee-colour.

"Oh, Fräulein Magnus!" Richard was ashamed of his nakedness and let himself drop into the water beside the steps. Now he was looking up at her, puffing and blowing. Her black bathing-costume absurdly reminded him of Susanne's dresses.

"Thanks," she said, "you've fairly splashed me." She made the water fly with her outstretched legs. "There, that's my revenge. But why are you staying in the water? Come on, let's sit down in the sun." She showed him no respect whatever.

She got up now. Her costume gleamed black and wet, her nipples stood out sharply, and the feminine triangle between her thighs was softly outlined.

"So your girl friend isn't here?"

"I beg your pardon?"

"Oh, the girl you have a mathematical flirtation with every day."

Richard came out sheepishly and sat down beside her on the sand. After he had buried his feet he felt less naked.

"I couldn't work if I didn't go in for sports," she said.

He could not help thinking a little contemptuously about Kapperbrunn: this was the kind of thing he had recommended. None the less Richard felt a touch of pride to think that he was proving as good a man now as Kapperbrunn. The incalculability of the world was once more manifest; the pinions of anarchy had touched him anew, and confronted with that black bathing-costume his thoughts revolved once more round Susanne. Ilse Nydhalm would certainly wear a white bathing-dress. The sky was becoming leaden. He said slowly:

"It's strange we haven't met before; I'm here almost every day."

"I'm generally here earlier than this."

She had taken off her white bathing-cap. Her hair was reddish-blond. Susanne's was almost black. And even Ilse Nydhalm's was dark.

All at once he saw it clearly: the sinful element in the world was the incalculable. Whatever was detached from causality and systematic relations, even though it might be nothing more than a forlorn sound vibrating in space, was sinful. An isolated event was senseless and sinful at the same time.

His ascetic face contracted.

Erna Magnus regarded him.

"If you took a little more exercise, too, it wouldn't do you any harm. You would be rather good-looking if you gave yourself a chance."

"Do you fancy that Gauss was a ski champion?" Usually he was not half so ready, but it was a retort he had inwardly employed against Kapperbrunn often enough, so that it lay on the tip of his tongue.

She laughed merrily.

"Are you coming to the university now?" she said.

The sound of church bells pealing rose forlorn in space and yet was not sinful, could not be sinful. Something wrong there with the argument, and yet there was nothing wrong, it was true enough: for, after all, Susanne's goings-on could not be called good, though on what grounds it was impossible for him to decide.

It seemed out of the question for him to appear at the university with Fräulein Magnus.

"No, I must go to the observatory."

"Surely you might show me over it sometime."

When she smiled, she showed all her teeth and a strip of gum. It was a mouth that had done a lot of kissing, that was certain. Hieck could not help thinking of the inn down in the wood below the observatory.

"Well, good-bye, Doctor Hieck."

She got up. She walked with a feminine swing of the hips.

Richard drew his feet out of the sand and lay on his back for a long time. With his fingers he raked the fine sand, which rustled lightly and got under his nails. He did his best to reinterpret what had happened, to touch it up: Erna Magnus was one of the physics students, her sexual characteristics ought therefore to be eliminated. But they were not eliminated. He flung an oblique glance upwards. On the diving-board stood a solitary figure, a young man with a gay cap on his head; arching his back, he stretched out his arms, sprang off the board, and shot down in an elegant curve. A second later one could hear the loud splash in the water.

Hieck did not arrive at the university until the afternoon.

Ilse Nydhalm said with thin lips:

"Fräulein Magnus has been here . . . I believe she was looking for you."

The only phrase that would come to Richard's mind was "snake in the grass." He said sheepishly:

"I met her anyhow earlier today."

Ilse Nydhalm did not reply but went on taking excerpts without lifting her nose.

They were silent. After a while he said:

"Would you like to have a look over the observatory sometime?"

Her grey eyes grew large.

"Really? May I?"

Richard left this time without having supervised the experimental work in the laboratory.

4

IF Katharine Hieck was fond of employing the phrase "I have no illusions left now," that was probably to be regarded as a reaction against an overdose of illusions and imagination, an overdose which was doubtless the result of her marriage to Hieck. For when she married him, her ideas of what was desirable and undesirable, praiseworthy and blameworthy, right and wrong, permitted and forbidden, were already firmly fixed; they had been determined by her peasant upbringing, were certainly older than her conscious thought, and were no longer to be shaken. But when she decided to marry Hieck—she could not understand yet how that had ever happened—she found herself in a completely different existence, which she had to interpret to fit her own ideals and which yet compelled her to tear herself away from all her firmly rooted notions. This had cost an enormous effort of imagination, almost beyond her powers, an effort which never indeed penetrated to her conscious mind, but yet was so excruciating that Katharine Hieck was driven to regard the confusion and darkness of her married life as a punishment for her betrayal of her own firmly established ideals, all the more so as the just apportionment of guilt and penance was included among these ideals. And she was accustomed to conclude such a train of thought with: "I have no illusions left now."

And since Karl Wohlfahrt had begun to come to the house, even her illusions about marrying again had ceased. She had found a sort of supplementary maternity; a feeling unburdened by any darkness in its origin, a more manageable feeling, so to speak, a franker motherliness than that which she could whip up, say, for Otto. Perhaps the peasant blood flowing in Karl's veins determined this elective affinity; perhaps this boy born in the country and condemned to live with his city-bred grandparents served her as an image of her own fate. However that may be, she pampered him on coffee and cakes.

Otto, who observed all this, was filled with jealousy and discomfort and fear over the course things were taking, but he held his peace.

On the other hand:

Karl had been promoted. He had been the first of the junior team to be included in the senior second eleven, and had been asked to play at the next friendly match with a rival club, the Stormy Petrels. With a lowering eye Otto invited his mother to go to see the match with him. She had never done so before. And Katharine Hieck curbed the dislike which she had for football and not only accepted the invitation but listened to Otto while he told her that Karl was the centre-half; indeed, that seemed to her a special distinction.

The first half of the game was over. The score stood at two to one for the Stormy Petrels.

Otto went round to the dressing-room as a matter of course. There was a great bustle there. On the benches in the wide central passage the players were sitting, some of them in that relaxed posture which they had learned from boxers on the cinema screens: legs widely outstretched and arms hanging limply. The cold sprays hissed in the shower-room. Ritter the trainer, a *præceptor Germaniæ* in a suit with large checks, was bellowing at the captain and the forwards for not combining properly. Werner Huschinski, the captain, was defending himself equally loudly. The Stormy Petrels, whose success had flown to their heads and who saw victory before them, were chaffing their hosts. Georg Bäcker had hurt his leg and was having it bandaged. In short, there was a great hustle. And Otto, proud to belong to it, though he was filled with envy of Karl, sniffed with dilated nostrils at the sharp sweat-impregnated air, in which were mingled the odours of rude health, underclothing, water, and lavatories.

Karl had pulled off his blue and yellow jersey, the colours of the Marathons. He was rubbing his back with a towel stretched tight between his two hands.

Ritter noticed Otto.

"Out you go; we don't want any hanging around."

Otto grinned and pointed to Karl. "I have to massage him." And he siezed the towel and began to pummel Karl's back.

The referee appeared in a white pullover and said, with all the dignity of an official personage:

"Interval's over. Be lined up in two minutes."

"Keep it up, Karl," said Otto, with professional goodwill, "and always pass to Krause when you're in a hole."

He went out, lit a cigarette with a grand gesture, and flung the match away with a grand gesture.

After the English fashion the teams appeared on the field at a run. Then applause sounded from the grandstand.

Frau Hieck was sitting in the grandstand. There were not very many people there: the officials of both clubs, who took a businesslike and secondary interest in the proceedings; then the usual young men in sports caps; and finally a number of comfortable middle-class gentlemen whom one might have expected to find anywhere but here, but who were driven by an inexplicable fate to an inexplicable enthusiasm for football and never missed a game. Frau Hieck found the unaccustomed spectacle exciting. She sat on her seat filled with curiosity and listened eagerly to Otto's explanations.

The game was now once more in full swing. The play was keener than in the first half. Immediately after the kick-off the Marathons had equalized the score, which now stood at two-all; things at once became serious. The two side-line men were kept busy; they ran to and fro; their white camp-stools remained unused. Every minute the ball was sent flying over the line. "Goal kick," Otto announced.

The flags at the corner posts fluttered. Karl ran past in his blue and yellow jersey. He was charged hard by a violet Stormy Petrel, fell, and remained lying. Frau Hieck cried out.

"It's all in the game," Otto calmly explained.

Meanwhile the other players had professionally worked Karl's legs up and down, and after a few breathing exercises he was set on his feet and with a clap on the back was sent into play again. The spectators dutifully applauded.

Frau Hieck was horrified.

"It's all in the game, is it? Have such things happened to you, too?"

But Otto was no longer listening. To her consternation she saw him begin to dance up and down, while at the same time he kept on yelling without a stop "Huschinski!" And it was not only he who was behaving so insanely, for the greater part of the crowd was seized by the same paroxysm, and meanwhile on the field itself things seemed to be happening just as urgently. The paroxysm mounted and mounted and ended in a general howl, amid which she could make out the incomprehensible word, "Goal, goal." Then all the excitement sank again with surprising quickness.

"It's out of the question, your taking part in this sort of thing again," said Frau Hieck decisively. "Such a horrible business!"

"Three-two for us," he said contentedly. "They'll never make it up . . . damnation! . . . Karl, hold him! . . ."

The yelling, though somewhat feebler, had begun again.

"What's wrong now?" asked Frau Hieck, now herself a little interested.

"Ouf . . . that was a close shave . . ."

The players were again charging towards the right, making for the Stormy Petrels' goal. The goal-keeper of the blue and yellows once more was lounging idly against a goal-post.

"Did you see Karl just now? . . . A first-rate pass!" Otto smiled half proudly, half maliciously at his mother.

"No," she was forced to admit; in the confusion she really could make out nothing.

So it went on for half an hour more, and when the whistle blew, the second eleven of the Marathons had won by four goals to two.

Frau Hieck travelled back by train; the two youths followed on their bicycles. They were received with a well-prepared and eloquently expressed admonition directed against football in general, expressing anxiety for the physical safety of the two youths in particular—for nothing good could come out of such brutality—and leading up to the example of Richard, who had never gone in much for sport. "Look at Richard, he has no time for such disgusting brutal games, and he's got on well enough." After his victory Karl had expected something different from this. Otto merely said: "Sport is sport," and Karl nodded.

Later, when they were alone together, Otto pointed casually at a chest of drawers. "That's where she keeps her money. Not a very safe place for it either, a chest of drawers."

After this his behaviour grew worse than ever. Every evening he disappeared. Unslept, with dark rings round his eyes, he slouched about all day, irritated at everybody and constantly on his guard.

5

RICHARD Hieck's dilemma was not inconsiderable. Erna Magnus had given him the idea of taking a visitor to the observatory, and actually it was with Ilse Nydhalm that he wanted to carry it out. On the horns of this dilemma almost two weeks went past. He solved it violently by proceeding to the observatory with Ilse Nydhalm alone. But he felt it as a breach of justice.

They neither of them felt very much at their ease, and question and answer alike remained within the confines of the astronomical. Already in the tram he had begun to expound Einstein's conception of the universe. She listened intently, but she also felt happy to think that they were conversing in a kind of secret language.

Opposite them was sitting a man with his legs straddling in the manner of corpulent people, reading a paper; from time to time he raised his grey-bearded face and glanced at them through his glasses. He was a kindly man, and he hesitated before he turned the pages of his paper, for he thought they were wanting to read the opposite side, while in reality they were merely comparing the universal comprehensibility of the newspaper with the isolation of their own specialized understanding. Hieck drew out a sheet of paper and proceeded to write down formulæ.

Dusk was already falling. Crowds were standing at the bathing-pool stop, waiting for the tram going back in the opposite direction. In passing Richard caught a glimpse of part of the surface of the pool over which rose the diving-tower, outlined sharply against the clear evening sky.

His conscience awoke anew. And in exculpation of something or other he said:

"Our observatories in Europe get very few nights when there is a clear sky . . . and so it's hardly worth our while to set up really expensive and first-rate instruments. . . . To-night, for a wonder, it's really clear enough to make good observations."

"Then I'm in luck," said Ilse Nydhalm.

"Yes," he said, and he was as proud of it as if he had made the weather conditions himself. "Besides, this is the season for shooting stars."

Thereupon Ilse Nydhalm said something unastronomical: "So we can make a wish."

From the night of memory broke a golden shaft. Miracle of desire, miracle of fulfilment, raised above the law, emerging from the void, falling back into the void, in its essence without shape, yet shining. Oh, man.

Hesitatingly, for he knew it was not in place, he said:

"It is probable that the craters in the moon were caused by gigantic meteorites."

When they arrived, the conductor had already switched on the lights, and the second tram stood brightly illuminated at the terminus. Two people were sitting in it.

The grey-bearded man with the newspaper lifted his hat to them and groaningly got off. Now he was disappearing into a dark tree-fringed side-street. Richard did not take the path through the wood, but the thoroughfare that wound up in two wide sweeps on the east side of the hill to the observatory.

From here they had a view of the city. Covered with a fume of mist like a layer of dust, the plain lay between the hill and the houses. The main boulevard ran straight towards the town; the lines of its tree-tops were dark, but between them the line of the paved road, illuminated by street lamps hidden among the foliage, glimmered fitfully like fluorescent rays. Down at the bathing-place the semicircle of cabins gleamed whitely, but the water-gleam of the pool was already melting into the misty air. The contours of the city, the spires of the cathedral, the spires of the university church and of the church of St. Anna, could still be distinguished; in rapid succession lights appeared in the massed houses, and here and there a few illuminated advertisement signs kept changing from yellow to red like wild-fire. The rows of street lamps ran straight out to the very edge of the town.

"Good visibility," said Richard, gazing up at the sky, in whose colourless vault the first stars showed themselves.

On the field adjoining the road straw ricks were standing; the field was dry, dry the bushes and trees at the turns of the road. Twilight lay on their night-clear faces.

Why is all this so important to us? thought Richard. Where is this life that rushes past us? Is it in this town? Does it fleet away to the skies up there?

"We'll be at the top in a minute," said Richard reassuringly, although Ilse must surely have known the road.

The hill was dominated by the cupola of the observatory, which made an unbroken line with the pine-clad heights.

Faded and dry and rigid. Almost warily the faded air lay upon and encompassed the rigidity of things.

Then they were at the top.

Richard showed Ilse his workroom. It was a quite ordinary room; it might very well have been the bureau of a tax official, but it pleased her.

"You've actually a sofa!"

Yes, a leather-covered sofa was standing there; he had never used it. And suddenly he felt uncomfortable and said:

"But now let's go and see the instruments."

"Splendid," said Ilse, putting on her glasses.

She had expected that he would conduct her straight away to the main refractor, that they would climb high up onto the tower, so as to behold at once as in a watchman's turret the thing she had come to see. But Richard Hieck had made up his mind to have a sytematic tour of inspection: through the classrooms first up to the meridian hall, then across to the refractor, while the route back would lead through the library. And so first they climbed the deserted stairs, passed through the meridian hall, which lay in silence and darkness, and from there stepped out on to a roof terrace.

"Here we have a comet-finder," said Richard, pointing to a shrouded instrument. "Of course this isn't quite up to date either."

It had become quite dark. They could see right over the tops of the pine trees, black outlines stabbing the darkness of space, out of which a soft wind came breathing. A flat rail-track was let into the concrete floor of the terrace.

Ilse would have liked to stay for a while on the terrace, but Hieck urged her away with strange impatience. Through a glass door they reached a narrow corridor, and then Hieck opened an ordinary-looking little door, and they were suddenly in the cupola—a slight shock, for they were not looking aloft but beneath them. They were standing in a little gallery and from there gazed down into a comparatively small, almost well-like space; and it was by no means a tower, for the iron framework of the cupola arched itself only at a moderate height. Before them they could see the slanting, gleaming powerful tubes of the refractor; down in the well was the observatory apparatus with the cushioned leather seat for the observer. The place smelt cool, dry, cellar-like.

A man was screwing and unscrewing at the complicated mechanism down there; it was not Professor Maier himself, as Hieck had actually expected, but Doctor Losska, the first assistant at the observatory.

"Good evening, Doctor Losska," said Richard. "May we come down?"

They descended the spiral stair from the gallery to the observer's stand.

Doctor Losska, a man with the permanently offended and drawn look of the neurotic, glanced up and half smiled. He had the sort of face which one might have expected at any moment to break into a nervous twitching. The absence of the twitching gave one an almost unpleasant feeling.

Richard Hieck introduced Ilse as a future astronomer.

"Good evening, Doctor Losska," said Ilse, holding out her hand. She laughed and blushed as she did so, for she had never until now thought of astronomy as a vocation; they had spoken of it for the first time on their way here. And a dim feeling awakened in her that now Richard had betrayed something which had been intended for him and him alone.

Losska wanted to say something agreeable, but somewhat missed the mark:

"It's hardly credible, the way women are getting in everywhere."

Ilse glanced at Richard, somewhat put out. But Richard had noticed nothing, and if he had noticed, he would have agreed with Losska. He was staring at the huge telescope as if he had never seen it before; he found the situation unexpectedly painful, and he regretted that he had brought Ilse here.

"Really it isn't a woman's job," said Ilse, looking shyly round the room. And after a short pause she added: "A pity."

No, it really wasn't a woman's job. Richard was quite of that opinion. And when Kapperbrunn called science women's work, it was absurd and nothing more than one of Kapperbrunn's paradoxical quips. Once for all, women students could not be regarded as women. Erna Magnus was simply an exception. Richard stared again at the refractor. If Erna Magnus had been here in Ilse's place, it would have been less painful. That was certainly a very disconcerting thought.

"Well, this is our main refractor," he said, expecting that Losska would now take up the conduct of the proceedings.

Instead of doing so, the assistant said:

"Strange to find you here. This is one of your free days, isn't it?" He had taken up the case containing the photographic plates and was looking irresolutely at it.

"One has no doubt to have a particular gift before one takes up astronomy," said Ilse. "It isn't enough merely to find it interesting."

Losska was flattered and unbent so far as to give a few explanations. He showed her the finder, the automatic swivelling-mechanism, and then he fell into the same half-ashamed local patriotism as Richard.

"A really modern apparatus would require an automatic observing-carriage too, of course."

"And you haven't one?"

"Huh!" Losska's tone was offended and contemptuous. Richard chimed in:

"And the cupola has to be moved by hand in this place."

The two men warmed to their theme. Losska rang for the attendant.

The cupola arched above them, brown and a little uncanny; the iron framework cast its shadows into the vault. Underneath its edge glittered a circular rail-line, over which it ran on rollers.

Losska drummed nervously with his fingers.

"Wherever can the attendant be?" he asked impatiently.

Richard said eagerly:

"I'd rather do it myself than wait for him."

But meanwhile Sauter, the fat attendant, had come in hurriedly, and with a somewhat contemptuous glance at the visitor began without further instructions to set a winch in the wall in rotation. The crack in the cupola gradually widened with a slight grinding sound. A strip of night-sky.

The refractor was directed straight at the crack.

Ilse gazed upwards. The strip of night-sky made her shiver. She did not know why.

"Everything in order, Herr Doktor?" asked Sauter, as he left.

"Yes, yes, Herr Sauter," murmured Losska, but Sauter was already outside.

Losska was now all alertness. His nervousness seemed to have fallen from him; he was in his element. Without even looking through the telescope, he manipulated the sights with his fingers—themselves a nervous and precise mechanism—and when everything was in order, he invited Ilse to take his place on the padded leather observation seat.

Ilse did so, her heart thudding.

"Do you see anything?" asked Losska.

Ilse saw a milky something with indeterminate edges, which seemed to be softly moving.

"Yes," she said rapturously.

Thereafter they left the telescope-room according to pro-gramme by the lower door and proceeded, accompanied by Losska, who for some inexplicable reason had joined them, across to the transit instrument.

"The position is not over-advantageous," explained Losska, "but the actual emplacement of the instrument is absolutely first-rate all the same." And against his usual custom he let himself go in a fairly long excursus on the vibration-free emplacement of astronomical instruments.

And as he was in such good form, he was preparing to add something on the inimical influence of temperature variations on the exactitude of one's observations and the measures for guarding against this, when Richard Hieck simply and blatantly interrupted him. Hieck suddenly found that Losska had already talked too much, both in general and about the apparatus of an observatory in particular, and that it was more than permissible and seemly that the talk should be guided back to the theoretical; consequently he began suddenly and in a loud voice to speak of the methods for calculating the distances of the stars, perfectly prepared also to clinch the matter with a practical illustration.

"You must excuse me, sir," said Losska, who now had become impatient in his turn, and who had actually to return to his post. "It's time for me to go."

"Oh, forgive me, we won't detain you," said Richard in confusion. "Fräulein Nydhalm must shortly be going too."

Losska's face seemed again on the verge of breaking into a nervous twitching. His little blue eyes surrounded with wrinkles looked with unfathomable animosity at the world, unfathomable his animosity, unfathomable his look, unfathomable the world.

Through the half-lit corridors, which reminded one of a sanatorium, they once more reached the official-looking workroom, where Richard had left his hat and Ilse's coat, and while he glanced for a second time over the papers laid out on his table, she leant, softly swaying, against the half-open door.

An extraordinary simplicity had been introduced into the world for Ilse Nydhalm—so it seemed to her. It was as though all the obscurity of the cosmos had been done away with; an order had supervened such as she with her twenty-one years had not yet imagined. It was as though everything had been a preparation for this moment. What had actually happened? Richard Hieck's expositions had made clear to her for the first time the cosmogony of the relativity theory—and now she remembered also the joy she had felt as a child when she had suddenly grasped what letters were, what reading meant. The ordering of the world in a new cosmogony! But conclusive as it seemed that this feeling of great and liberating order flowed from such knowledge and the consciousness of such knowledge, there existed along with it a gentler and yet mightier intuition, also with roots striking into the opaque being of childhood, an intuition over which hung the trees of a long-forgotten garden, a reminiscent knowledge which did not need the macrocosm of astronomy in order to reach the microcosm of the soul, but rather took the opposite path, confining what was essential in the world's happenings to an extraordinarily small point in the present: to be standing there in a bright new summer dress, leaning lightly against a door, a breathing young human being with a place in the happenings of the world, the breathings of the stars, the heart-beat of the future. Oh, woman.

They stepped out into the road. Richard had resumed his lecture and now dilated on Einstein's hypothesis of curved space, the expansion and contraction of which determined the motions of the great stellar systems.

Ilse listened and did not listen; she understood all and understood far more at the same time. The state in which she found herself was one of manifold knowledge, as it were: when Richard spoke of the geometrical possibilities and difficulties of that most radical of spatial hypotheses, her mind was wide open to what he said and yet she knew that here the cosmos was concerned in achieving something that had very little to do with mathematical formulations, something that lay, supercosmic and mighty, behind all possibility of precise expression and whose presence was possibly more evident to her than exact astronomical space. There was nothing astrological or mystical in it, and although the terrifying hypothesis of a firmament that expanded and contracted again brought near to her the similitude of human breathing, yet it was more than an external similitude if Ilse Nydhalm now with every breath she drew felt the indissoluble relation between what was thought and experienced, what could be thought and experienced, as a new and wonderful harmony of her whole being; for the knowledge by means of which this happened floated like a manifold echo in the vault of Being, and the words which bore it, the voice on which the words were borne, floated in the vessels of the spheres and yet in her too.

A soft thoughtful furrow had again formed between her brows, and Ilse Nydhalm said:

"Really it's terrifying that a man should actually have discovered and thought out all that."

But beyond all the awful terror of thought there floated, still more terrifying, the second significance of the world, scarcely to be grasped at all, expressible neither in mathematical formulæ nor in words, yet uplifted high above all terror, an extraordinary coolness, mobility, and freedom of the brain, an exciting transposition into a reality of another order which corresponded to nothing else and yet bore within it the evidence of consummate truth. It was like a blissful trance of contemplation.

Now and then twigs snapped in the darkness that soundlessly brooded over the woods.

Ilse Nydhalm said:

"And it's so dreadfully still . . . but that's what makes it so lovely, too."

Richard Hieck had now come to the connexion between the minutest part of non-Euclidian space and non-Euclidian space as a whole. He did not like interruptions. Even though he meant something else by his expositions. Or for that very reason. He spoke on.

She smiled, a little touched by his enthusiasm, almost grateful that he did not let himself be held up, that he insisted on this form of communication and that it remained in doubt whether the manifold meaning of the world lay in things themselves, or in the way in which he presented them, or in the mood to which one listened to them. His voice sounded a little hoarse and subdued, not so arrogant as in the classroom; it was a voice of human knowledge, environed with darkness, lacing itself round the boughs of darkness.

117

The trees of childhood bend over every night, and ever again sounds the forgotten voice, the forgotten voice of security.

And as if the wide-open night, as if the blissful contemplation of the manifold, had now become manifest to him as well, Richard stumbled in his harangue and stopped in astonishment, clapping on his head the stiff old straw hat which he had been carrying in his hand. Something or other did not fit; he felt half ashamed of his behaviour, half ashamed of his lecture—his impatient ascetic face contracted painfully; it was the shame of insufficiency that had seized him. For a moment he could not help thinking of the bathing-pool. But that was different. For a moment he could hear his mother's clear voice. The essential was inexpressible. The final truth and the deepest sin, frontiers of the word. He gazed out into the dark plain; he avoided Ilse's eyes.

Love.

Suddenly the word came into his mind, filling him with terror. But he was unable to combine it with any image. Vaguely he thought of human couplings, thought still more darkly that he himself had already collaborated in such things; simultaneously there came into his mind the image of Susanne, who had renounced all love—that was at least clearly understandable—and the night-sky gleamed black like a wet bathing-dress. No connexion with what was actually happening here, although the planes of knowledge lay quite close together, and one always believed that the one could be reached from the other. The word remained isolated, without connexion. Ilse's dress gleamed brightly in the darkness.

Love.

Suddenly the word was there, and Ilse Nydhalm started so violently that it vanished again.

A forlorn sound, locked within itself.

118

Alarmed, Richard Hieck pulled himelf together. And he began once more to speak of his own affairs and of the aim that impelled him: to seize the whole world in the mirror of mathematics. He spoke on of himself, of himself alone, and yet it was a flight, a flight from his blind individual being into a greater one, yet also a flight back into that individual being and the burning core of its will; it was at once a rejection of the you and a surrender of the I. And when they reached the silent inn among the trees, where only a lonely light behind the garret window was burning now, he said something that he had never formulated before, that he had never even been aware of before:

"The man who achieves such knowledge that he can understand the whole universal process will be immortal . . . I mean inwardly immortal."

Immediately afterwards he felt ashamed.

"Shall we sit down for a minute?" he said, indicating the dark menacing flotilla of tables and benches.

The clearing lay before them filled with motionless hot air, encompassed by the immobile pine woods. But a wall of cloud was advancing from the north between them and the starry vault.

"A shooting star!" cried Ilse.

Richard had not noticed it; he looked at the clouds.

"We can't stay here; there's thunder in that cloud."

It was a motionless cloud of pine fragrance that they walked down through, and Ilse said:

"I wished a wish . . ." and as he waited in expectant silence, she added awkwardly: ". . . that you should achieve that immortality." It sounded rather like the ceremonial wishes that she had recited once upon a time on her father's birthday, except that it was a little warmer, and she was half afraid that Richard Hieck would now paternally take her in his arms, as her father had done. But he accepted the wish without a word of thanks; it was all too near his own wish,

119

and it was impious to put it into words. Unutterable lay the crystalline landscape of death and immortality; no word could ever come near it. And Richard sighed, barely audible. They went on in silence.

When they emerged from the woods, summer lightning was silently playing on the horizon. But by the time they had reached the tram car, the storm was already whistling in the trees along the boulevard and the lightning was flashing, followed at ever shorter intervals by the thunder.

Ilse laughed.

"Just in the nick of time!"

During the clattering journey they did not hear the thunder, but every now and then the plain was whitely illuminated, an immense dish ready to receive the rain and the rumbling flash. Expectation and fulfilment of the impending.

"A storm like that does one good in this awful heat," said the conductor, who had planked himself in front of them and balanced himself in rhythm to the rolling of the tram. It was nice of the man to talk to them.

Then a crowd of people got in with dripping hats and wet patches on their shoulders. And everyone who got in spoke of the thunderstorm and of the rain, which was already abating. And right enough, in the town the rain was almost over. Swift little streams of water were rushing alongside the pavements down to the canal railings, where they plunged in. Richard escorted Ilse Nydhalm home; she had put on her white summer coat.

6

IT was Sunday, and the morning air was liquid and golden clear; it tasted light and pleasant. But Otto, who was still lying in bed, had no taste for it. He had a bad head, he felt hot, and his naked feet were sticking out from beneath the blankets.

Susanne came in.

"When on earth are you coming for your breakfast?"

"Let me sleep." Otto sighed.

She stood beside his bed, regarded his lightly tanned body, and felt a little touched. Otto stretched out one foot towards her.

"No wonder you're tired; do you think I don't know when you come home at night?"

"Oh, if Richard has told you, then you do know, I suppose."

He had come home later than Richard for three nights running now. And each time there had been a row.

"Can't I have my coffee here?" he asked coaxingly.

"No, we're not going to start that," Susanne decided. "Anyone who wants his breakfast must get up for it."

Otto stretched himself.

"Oh, I wish you'd move to that lousy convent of yours."

Half clothed, unwashed, uncombed, he appeared in the living-room. He said in a whining voice:

"What a lovely day."

"I suppose that's why you don't get up?" Without waistcoat or jacket, his feet in slippers, Richard was sitting in his white Sunday shirt like the master of the house, reading the diocesan weekly to which Susanne subscribed.

Otto said venomously:

"Yes, that's why I don't get up."

"I can't see why," said Susanne.

"Because on a day like this all the fellows are away on their motor-bikes."

"And you haven't got one?" commented Richard. "Queer."

"You big fathead," shouted Otto, "it's all very well for you to talk!" He had jumped up, his roll in his hand. "A fat fool like yourself gadding about with your girls in the university . . . it's easy for you to talk . . . you have an easy time of it."

Now Richard had no wish to become angry, but it was extremely painful to him to have the mere possibility of any relation with a girl mentioned in Susanne's presence; it seemed to him as if he were being accused, and not even with injustice, of an act of infidelity, and so he said:

"Hold your tongue, for goodness' sake, Otto; you're being tiresome."

"Come, Otto, be a good boy," Susanne seconded him.

Otto was not disposed to give up his ravings; he was in the mood and had not yet played his best trump cards.

"You . . . both of you do what pleases you . . . but I . . . have I been allowed to paint . . . what?"

Frau Hieck came out of the kitchen.

"What's wrong here?"

The sight of his mother drove Otto quite beyond himself. "Everything's all wrong . . . I wish I was dead."

Forlorn the sound of death, even when it is uttered by a childish and hysterical voice. And Richard let fly:

"That's enough now of your childish showing-off. Fool! Idiot!"

"Will you be good enough to tell me what all this is about?" Frau Hieck's clear, purling voice too was not exactly lowered. Fair and young she stood there among these dark creatures who were her children, and she had planted her hands on her haunches.

"Otto, why are you shouting there like a madman?"

"We'll have to shut the windows, or else we'll have the whole street here," said Susanne.

There was a strip of ivy growing along the side of the window; its leaves glistened in the bright sunlight. "It's no business of yours what I'm doing, it isn't!" Otto spat at his mother.

The presence of evil and madness in the world is instantaneous, like a miracle, meteorlike it plunges into life, bearing death in it, irremediable by thought.

"Have you done anything to him, Richard?" asked Katharine Hieck. She had a feeling as though now her last and nearest child were wanting to slip away from her into the fields of darkness from which he came. And yet she could not take that seriously; none of them could be completely lost, even at the other end of the world.

Richard laughed.

"No, I've done nothing to the young man."

"Otto, be a good lad." Frau Hieck assumed her wheedling voice and tried to draw Otto's face to her.

"The good lad wants a motor-bike," growled Richard.

"No, what an idea!" Frau Hieck was astonished. "But you have your bicycle. You were thinking of taking a run into the country with it today. Come, be a good boy, Otto; if Karl were to hear how you're going on, you'd feel properly ashamed . . ."

That was the last straw. Indignant, horrified, hostile, Otto stared at his mother and rushed from the room.

The others were left with the uncomfortable feeling of being responsible for a fate which, though part of their common fate and nurtured from the same sources, had yet sundered itself from them and was going its own way to its own doom. But because that way led through the same darkness, they felt offended and annoyed.

"What a fool!" said Richard, taking up his diocesan news again.

"Has he taken his breakfast at least?" asked Katharine Hieck.

"You can be easy in your mind about that."

Katharine Hieck laughed, relieved.

"What girls are there at the university?" Susanne's voice was heard.

A little more, and Richard would have rushed out of the room in just as furious a rage as his young brother. So he merely said:

"I'll have a look to see what the young fool is doing."

In her light dress and her white apron Katharine Hieck stood by the side of her grim daughter.

"Could you give Karl Wohlfahrt one or two evening lessons in mathematics, do you think? . . . You know, Otto's friend."

"Yes, why not?" Richard left the room, walking stiffly in his soft felt slippers, one shoulder raised a little higher than the other.

Otto was standing at the wash-stand with his head stuck in the basin and blowing lustily.

"Well, well," said Richard, putting his foot up on a chair and beginning to lace his shoes.

This happened in the forenoon. In the afternoon Karl Wohlfahrt appeared and was greeted by Otto with the utmost cordiality.

IV

1

KRISPIN announced with satisfaction:

"Fräulein Magnus says she's going off tomorrow."

Of course; her work was pretty well finished. Hieck went up to the laboratory.

Erna Magnus was sitting over her diagrams.

"Well, there we are; enough material for a thesis. Don't you think so?"

Richard was disconcerted because she was wearing not the usual smock but a red, and as it seemed to him, fragrant summer frock. And it was somehow beyond his comprehension that this young lady should have anything to do with the charges of electrons.

"Well, Doctor Hieck, have you been thinking about that visit of ours to the observatory?"

"Fräulein Magnus . . ." began Richard.

"Oh, yes, I know you couldn't arrange it before, but I'm on the spot now." She looked at him mirthfully.

He cast an oblique glance upwards. Why did he suddenly think of Hilda Wasmuth?

"Are you going off to the mountains?" he tried to turn the conversation. The mountains that Erna Magnus was to favour with her presence would undoubtedly be higher, more adventurous, and more fashionable than those where Kapperbrunn was holidaying. And between the life that so incomprehensibly roared along these mountain torrents and the abstract life of the university Erna Magnus formed a connecting link, bringing them into strange association with each other, a very strange association that included even Susanne's room.

"Are you relieved to be getting rid of me?"

Yes, he was relieved at the prospect. And yet she would be taking away something that he could not put into words at the moment. And so it was no lie when he said:

"Not at all."

She said with great good-humour:

"Well, you've had enough of being tormented by me," but she could not refrain from adding: "Ilse Nydhalm's easier to get on with, isn't she?"

Of course he was annoyed by these direct insinuations, but they flattered him, too; indeed from some aspect or other which he preferred to ignore they were actually important, for they endowed Ilse Nydhalm with a femininity that Erna Magnus had first taught him to see. Sometimes it really seemed that Erna Magnus's presence in the university had brought a new note into it, a note of sheer femininity that changed the community of women students into a kind of sisterhood and released them from the fixity of their sexlessness. A kind of sisterly recognition that encouraged Ilse Nydhalm, too.

All the same he had to take the sting out of these insinuations.

"But Fräulein Nydhalm's work is quite different from yours."

"I'm sure of that." Erna Magnus gave a low, warm laugh. She was taking a pair of lovers under her protection; she was a real woman.

Her laugh suddenly stood isolated in space, and Richard was reminded of a chemical or physical catalytic agent, which remains unaffected by certain reactions but must be present if the reactions are to take place at all.

So he stuck to his theme.

"Fräulein Nydhalm will need the whole of the vacation to finish sorting the papers."

"Yes, that's right, don't be in too much of a hurry."

To approve and forbid, these were really Susanne's functions, and her jurisdiction would widen again once Erna Magnus was gone. This idea, too, disconcerted Richard, and so he closed the conversation gruffly:

"Then I can only wish you a pleasant journey."

She twinkled at him:

"And I hope you have a good time over your work."

A person who has seen another naked is permitted to be ironical, so he let her irony pass. But again Susanne came into his mind, when she added: "Well, then, *auf Wiedersehen* in the autumn."

Would Susanne be able to fill her place? Would that terrible and incomprehensible thing called life come within his reach again in the autumn term? In half an hour's time Erna Magnus would have left the university, and he did not know why that upset him so much. The symbol of the catalytic agent explained nothing, it was no theory; his need for building theories remained unsatisfied. With a feeling of dejection he picked up the folder containing the results of Erna Magnus's work.

"Yes, *auf Wiedersehen* in the autumn."

The folder under his arm, one shoulder drawn up higher than the other, he walked with his stiff, somewhat heavy step across to Weitprecht's department.

"*Wiedersehen*, Doctor Hieck," came echoing after him.

Now Krispin would start on the great annual clean-up in the laboratory.

The sky looked pale through the corridor windows; a windy August day, already charged with the coolness of autumn; the blue of the sky was changing imperceptibly into a veil of bright cloud.

Richard was almost amazed when he came on Ilse Nydhalm. She was sitting at Weitprecht's desk, her hands folded, her eyes fixed on vacancy. Before her lay the usual pile of papers.

Bright, bare, and cool the wind-blown day came in through the panes of glass, sometimes varied by bursts of golden sunlight. Richard felt forlorn and naked beneath his clothes.

But she gave him a smile as he came in, and then she put on her spectacles and bent over her work. That she was only making a pretence of working, while actually she was making hay of the papers—that, at any rate, escaped Richard's notice. But he saw the helpless, short-sighted look with which she peered at the manuscript, and he could not help thinking of blindness. That touched him. And it was a comfort to him that she was wearing her hygienic white smock. But she was not wearing a tie; round her bare throat hung a chain of great amber-coloured beads.

"Fräulein Magnus has finished her job," he said, indicating the folder, which he laid on the table. "Weitprecht will be pleased."

"Yes," she said, studying the cover of the folder; "Experimental Series D-G" was written on it, and underneath in brackets: "Erna Magnus."

A current of unknown life came surging in from somewhere, a current from some as yet unknown source of evidence which might hold the real meaning of everything, even of mathematics. For the purpose of knowledge lies outside knowledge.

Outside the university buildings, at all events.

"Shall I open the window?" he asked, and immediately opened it. The result was a puff of wind that whirled into disorder the papers on the table; a few sheets sailed down on to the floor.

"Ugh," said Richard resentfully, beginning to pick them

130

up, but hardly had he secured them when the wind swept a second detachment on to the floor. Now Ilse, too, had come to the rescue. And every time she stooped, the amber beads slid out of the hollow in her neck and dangled before her chin.

It was hopeless to struggle against the wind. Richard finally recognized the fact and said:

"We'll have to shut the window."

Side by side they stood at the window. Down below, a car was passing by. The newspaper shop over the way—proprietress Sidonie Metzinger—had picture postcards hung up all over its door. The windows of the small millinery establishment beside it had the usual three hats on show. A girl issued from a house-door, battling against the wind, holding her fluttering skirts around her. Paper and dust went helter-skelter over the asphalt and lay piled in undulating drifts.

Was Erna Magnus still in the university buildings?

Somewhere or other life was roaring along, dark, unending, unattainable, incomprehensible.

A dark cloud, that is our past; out of the sea of darkness we are lifted up on the flood and hurled into blind solitude. Here is the farthest limit of desire, and what is bright and clear is sucked back again into the wave of what has been. Her voice trembling, Ilse said: "Yes, now we can go on working," and in the next breath she was sobbing, leaning against him. With his lips on her hair he held her in an awkward embrace.

Among the picture postcards at the door of the newspaper shop hung the notification of someone's death. A dog at the corner lifted a leg. A car with a black-lacquered roof, its ventilator open, glided past. From a window of one of the houses opposite a woman was leaning out; she had a leathery yellow face, a black dress; she was resting her fat bare arms on the windowsill and gazing down into the street. The smoke from a chimney blew on to the roof-tiles, was dispersed and carried off by the wind.

But now Ilse saw the woman across the street, and drew away from the window. And as if she had nothing more pressing to do than to get on with her work, she picked up her red pencil by the wrong end and began to scramble wildly through her papers. Her slim body was shaking, a tear fell on the paper, and Richard, standing beside her in complete confusion, remembered that Otto had sobbed in the same still manner. He twitched out his handkerchief to wipe the tear-drop from Weitprecht's paper.

At that, she looked up into his painfully contracted, ascetic face, and only then, as an almost imperceptible smile hovered, unknown to herself, around her lips, did their faces find each other in an awkward kiss, released from all willing, released from Being, upborne by the wave of darkness that washed over them.

Forlorn note of solitariness, forlorn note of death.

It was without desire. It was more than desire. It was utter surrender and panic. It was no rapture. It was more than rapture. It was an uplifting out of the sea; it was the poised moment on the crest of the wave, open to the sun and wind that play over the darkness. It was not despair. It was more than despair. It was a Being torn from the weft of Becoming, from the mother-and-sister weft of blind slumber; it was the shudder of freedom, the spectre of noon, that touched them. Oh, fear of brightness, fear of the midday sun.

Somewhere in the building a door shut with a bang.

They looked at each other. And then they tried to tidy up. And smiled to each other. Laid things the wrong way round. Took each other by the hand. Put Erna Magnus's diagrams in the cabinet. Said nothing. And were as if a judgment had descended upon them. And smiled in spite of it. And laid the pencils in the glass tray. And he bent over her hair and kissed it.

And without having come to any arrangement, he left the building before her, to keep Krispin the attendant from guessing anything.

Richard Hieck went home, and yet he was not going home. He went over to the little paper shop and studied the death notice and the picture postcards, and he cast a glance at the three hats in the milliner's. He walked through the town and gazed at the diamonds on their black velvet background in the jewellers' windows. He stood by the parapet of the bridge and looked for something on the blind surface of the smooth-flowing, bottle-green water. Something dark was flowing in himself, carrying him along; and he did not want to see Susanne.

Ilse Nydhalm went home, and yet she was not going home. She felt very wideawake, although she was probably anything but that. She peered at all the faces she met to see if one of them had an ascetic look. She did pass several gentlemen who were clumsy and bulky and walked secretively, but she did not notice them. She was downcast, and yet her dejection had something bright, almost solemn and festal, in it. And suddenly gloriously, beating its wings and yet sinking frightful claws into her, there swooped upon her heart the word: Love.

The wind in the streets had died down; it had become oppressively sultry again, as befitted a day in the beginning of August.

2

WHEN old Haubigl had first entered the commercial art studio, engraving on copper and such-like was still being done there. He was as old as that. He was a skilled line-engraver and was teaching Otto his craft.

Bending over the copper-plate, the needle in his hand, Otto sat at the long oak working-bench in front of the large, sloping window of the studio. Haubigl was peering with satisfaction over his shoulder; it was an unsual commission that the studio had received: a menu card in the old-fashioned style for a fashionable restaurant—a wreathed garland of cooked meats, flowers, and champagne bottles, the whole topped by a luxuriant epergne crowned with fruit. And had old Haubigl not been there, the studio would have had to refuse the commission. That Otto was being allowed to work on it was an extraordinary privilege.

"You'll make a better artist yet than the blockheads of the Academy."

Otto, without looking up, shook his head.

"Not me, I'm done for," he said dramatically.

Haubigl, with his old, thick-veined, yellow hands, his delicate, aristocratic-looking nails rimmed with black, turned the boy round, revolving-chair and all, to face him.

"Listen to me, old Papa Haubigl doesn't care for that kind of talk; anyhow, for a long time I haven't liked the way you've been going on."

It was a stubble-grown face, with faded lips and faded eyes, yet a face with a keen look behind the steel spectacles, into which Otto found himself looking.

134

"Well, what's troubling you, son?"

Otto made the answer that every boy makes in the circumstances:

"Nothing."

"Too many high jinks?"

"I haven't the money for that." With an obstinate expression he slid down from the chair.

Haubigl patted him kindly on the shoulder. "Well, go and have a wash, it's long past four."

Dumbly Otto went over to the wall-tap, took off his blue working blouse, washed and slipped into his jacket. He would have liked to speak, but something was choking in his throat. Besides, what could he have said? There was absolutely nothing at all.

"Good night, Herr Haubigl."

"Good night, my boy."

Otto took his bicycle from the bicycle-stand in the yard and raced off. When he got home, he stole cautiously up the stair, cautiously into the house, and then burst suddenly into his mother's room as if to catch someone napping.

"Is Karl here?"

"No," she responded quietly, "but he may be waiting in your room."

That was both a disappointment and a relief. And both feelings strengthened when he found that Karl was not in his room either. He came back to his mother.

"He's not there. Hasn't he really turned up?"

"Not so far as I know . . . what do you keep fiddling round the chest of drawers for?"

"Nothing, I only thought it was standing open. . . ."

In about half an hour's time Karl really did turn up; he was welcomed by Otto with the guileful remark:

"You've been here once already looking for me, says Mother."

He watched Karl's eyes, to see if they had any especially glad and satisfied expression.

"No," said Karl, "this is the first time I've been here today."

Perhaps Karl only wanted to conceal the fact that he had the money? Then in God's name let him keep it. Otto wanted nothing more to do with the money; he was fed up with it, but he must know how things stood, and he would manage to get that out of Karl, surely.

"You know, I don't really need any money now. Haubigl thinks I'll soon be a great artist; then I'll earn money hand over fist."

It appeared, however, that he could get no more out of Karl than out of his mother. Karl was giving nothing away. And whether his mother had missed any money simply could not be ascertained, in spite of all Otto's hints and roundabout inquiries. His suspicion grew that she had given it to Karl and that they were both concealing the fact. What had happened between the two of them? Otto was brought up before a blank wall and had the feeling that he must dash his head to pieces against it.

Karl said:

"Your brother's going to give me some coaching in mathematics. Today is my first lesson."

"That's queer," said Otto suspiciously.

"How is it queer?"

"Because nobody's said a word to me about it." This was not completely true, for Richard had asked him several questions about Karl. Yet that had been more than a week ago. And Richard had been so patently preoccupied by other matters that his questions had not sounded as if they were made in earnest. For about a week Richard had been altogether unaccountable in his behaviour; he had quite changed—Otto's observant eye had of course noticed the change—not only had there been no more rows about coming home late at night, but there was no doubt that Richard was taking up in general a passive attitude of brotherly comradeship. He has something on his conscience, thought Otto. But what good was that to anybody?

Richard came in. Karl was introduced and taken off to be cross-examined.

Meanwhile Otto sat beside his mother in the kitchen. On the gas stove a great pan was bubbling. Otto could smell the apricots that were being turned into jam. His mother had her sleeves rolled up and was peeling and stoning the fruit. In a green earthenware bowl the halved apricots lay ready for cooking.

Otto slowly fished one after another out of the bowl. While he sat eating them, he again felt inclined to burst into tears. Why was there no going back? Why did he have to dash his head against a wall that no one had told him to raise? Something he could not name had him in its grip, but he guessed that it was an opponent of everything he saw around him, of all that he was actually now seeing as if for the first time: the slow, regular movement of his mother's arms, the regular fall of the apricots into the bowl. It was really the first time he had ever looked at this kitchen, the utensils hanging on the tall dresser; he went over each of them by name—the egg-whisk, the skimming-ladle, the row of wooden cooking-spoons—and while at the same time he was wondering why he had never tried to draw them, he was overwhelmed by an enormous pity for himself and an enormous weight of apprehension. What cruel and terrible power had seized hold of him, what power hostile to all this domesticity? Alas, it was simply life that had him in its grip, life in itself, the most terrible power to which the human being is subject, and there is no use sighing over it. But Otto did not know that, he hardly even guessed it, and so he was sorry for himself and heaved a sigh.

Reproachfully he said:

"Why have you arranged special lessons for Karl?"

Katharine Hieck looked up.

"If you eat so many apricots you'll have a pain."

Otto went out of the kitchen in a huff, and although he made a quick snatch for a last apricot, he was even more deeply offended than he believed. And while the soft-fleshed fruit shredded away to nothing in his moouth, he felt that he was an outcast. Yes, cast out, that was it. He had not even a room to stay in. Richard was sitting in his room cheek by jowl with Karl. Horrible.

Karl had just come to an end of his examination and was saying: "Thank you."

"Are you going to stay?" asked Otto.

"No, I've got to go home."

That was a good thing. All the same, it wasn't certain that he mightn't sneak back in the night-time.

And as if to prove that this was possible, Katharine Hieck asked during supper:

"Well, how did you get on with Karl, are you going to give him lessons?"

"Of course there's ever so much he can't do," said Richard. "That's all because of this damned football. I'll send him to a woman student I know."

"But he's a good player," said Otto, roused to opposition. "Isn't that so, Mother, Karl's a good player?"

"I know nothing about it, but if you say he is, I'm ready to believe you."

"He's the best half-back on the team," insisted Otto.

"What woman student do you mean?" asked Susanne.

"Oh, it doesn't matter," said Richard. "Ilse Nydhalm's her name."

"He doesn't need any extra lessons," burst out Otto.

"If he's willing to learn more, that's all to his credit," said his mother.

Richard decided:

"I fancy that I'm quite capable of judging whether he needs to be coached or not."

Otto had the feeling that they were all leagued against him. Wherever they could, they sided with each other against him. He was an outcast. What language did they speak? Their lips moved and they came to an understanding with each other through the words that came out of their mouths. But as for him, he could no longer get them to understand his meaning. Were they blind to what was going on?

"You're not eating anything," said his mother, setting up to be sanctimonious.

"Can't, I'm not hungry."

"Yes, I thought you'd eaten too many apricots."

That was his mother! And Susanne? She was always raving about loving one's neighbor like a Christian, and yet there she sat shoving food into herself as stodgily as the others. Otto made a last attempt:

"Susanne."

"Yes."

"Susanne, I'd like to go to confession."

Susanne pricked up her ears.

"What . . . is that true?"

Richard cast an oblique glance at her.

"You've heard that he's just been overeating himself on apricots. You should know him by this time."

Susanne felt injured.

"If you're trying to make a fool of me, Otto, I won't speak to you again. These are sacred things."

"I've had enough of all of you," said Otto. "I'm going to sleep now."

He could hear his mother's comment:

"Now he really has a pain."

When Richard later came into the bedroom they shared, Otto was lying on his bed. He was still dressed, only his shirt was open in front. With a strangely unyouthful face he lay there, and his breast rose and fell beneath his open shirt. Richard felt almost disquieted as he looked at him. Otto sat up.

"Richard," he said in a tense voice, "Mother . . ."

"Well, what about Mother?"

"Mother's taken Karl under her wing."

Now it was out, expressed with as little emphasis as possible, but still it was out.

"Well, what do you need to care . . . ?"

Otto sprang up.

"Of course . . . you don't give a button for me . . ."

"Have you gone off your head, Otto?"

"It's all very well for you . . . you only want Karl to get lessons . . . you and your Fräulein Nydhalm."

Richard felt helpless.

"I thought you said you were going to sleep."

"I'll go to sleep if I like . . . and I'll go to the café now if I like."

Richard said nothing. This was too much. And he was almost glad to see the boy take his impudent face out of the room. He sat down to work.

That Otto should turn back half-way and spend half the night stalking round the house, that, of course, was something no one could have predicted.

3

SOME difficulties had to be obviated before Karl's private tuition could be got under way, and Richard, who had his share of the family guilefulness, had foreseen them: it was as little possible for him to introduce Karl Wohlfahrt into a strict house like Ilse Nydhalm's as it was for himself to visit her there, and since Ilse could not be expected to go to Karl's house, there was nothing for it but to make the Hieck dwelling the scene of their encounters.

But that was what Richard was aiming at; he did not tell himself so, but his desire to show Ilse to his sister Susanne had been growing stronger ever since Erna Magnus went away.

Katharine Hieck regarded Ilse with jealous eyes. Somehow she had an inkling that this might be a daughter-in-law, and that a new generation was growing up to conspire against her, a generation to which Karl belonged, too.

Instinctively she appealed to Susanne.

"Do you think they're having an affair?" she asked naïvely, and Susanne, with a superior tone, as if she were the elder, gave the required answer: "Of course; any child could see it; they're all like that at the university." True, she did not herself believe what she said.

Richard, however, was by no means having an affair with Ilse. He saw her in the university as before; he called to take her to her coaching-lessons and escorted her home again, but almost vehemently he avoided meeting her on any other occasion, almost vehemently he confined himself to mathematics and physics, permitting no deviation from scientific themes and holding forth on these as usual. And he grew irritable when he fancied that she was not listening with the same attention as formerly.

Why was this so? Was it perhaps because of the contempt that Susanne openly displayed whenever Ilse Nydhalm was mentioned? It was not that she despised Richard's lack of morals, as one might have expected; quite the contrary, she let him understand in no ambiguous terms that his immoral relations with Ilse need not be concealed from her. But that he, whose ideals she had always respected and with whom she had always associated on equal terms, should descend to an affair with "a creature of that kind," that was enough to provoke her keenest, most contemptuous disparagement. "A creature of that kind," not a woman at all, simply a student. No good for anything, neither for working like a decent woman nor going into a decent man's bed, and least of all could she be of any good to God. Susanne did not mince matters, and although Richard told himself that the opinion of such an idiotic person should not concern him, he could not help thinking of Erna Magnus—Susanne wouldn't have been able to sneer at her. He thought of the black bathing-costume that Erna Magnus had worn. He thought of Hilde Wasmuth. He did his best to recall to mind the various low-class adventures he had had with women whom he found it difficult to remember. And he was convinced that Susanne would have tolerated any of them rather than just Ilse Nydhalm. One only had to look at Susanne: the way she sat there, imperturbable in her black dress, surrounded by her holy pictures, her face severe above her too fat body; and when she cast an oblique glance upwards, showing the whites of her eyes, and smiled secretively over something that remained incomprehensible to everybody else, one could not help understanding this at least, that Ilse Nydhalm would never find favour in her eyes.

142

From Susanne's viewpoint "a creature of that kind" was just about good enough to give lessons to Karl.

And so in a way it was a triumph for Susanne's authority to have Ilse Nydhalm degraded to being a governess, but that escaped both Ilse's notice and Richard's. Ilse's especially, for she enjoyed these lessons; she wanted to shine before Richard; her ambition was spurred on to develop all the mathematical talents in her pupil, and so in the end Karl Wohlfahrt had to suffer because of the strange mechanism that Richard had set a-going between Susanne and Ilse.

Little as Richard understood this mechanism, however, he felt that he still owed a debt to love and to Ilse Nydhalm, and that it could not be paid in mathematical coinage, not even though Ilse adapted her conversation to his and set herself to the task of building together with him a mathematical world in which he could be king. It was no world that could compare with Susanne's; it was, indeed, no world at all, but at most a small, isolated, and therefore sinful community of understanding. And as he exerted himself none the less to build this world for and with Ilse Nydhalm, he came to the conclusion that love, or what he took to be love, was like a curve stretching into infinity, constantly approaching the infinite but never actually reaching it. And all efforts to achieve this hopeless task were at the same time an attempt to pay off the unknown debt to love or to Ilse—in this respect they were one and the same—to win Ilse's forgiveness for something that was as far beyond him to express as the simple word love.

The days were growing shorter. It was still warm weather. In the pale-blue evening sky there stood black, silver-rimmed clouds. Motionless.

Into the darkening sitting-room, where Ilse and Karl did their lessons, came Katharine Hieck.

"You might as well stop for today; it's getting dark."

"Rather," said Karl in glee, shutting his copy-book.

Katharine Hieck bent over the table on which the school-books and copy-books were strewn and stroked Karl's fair curly head. He flushed and paled, but nobody noticed that, for it was already too dark.

"Must we really stop now? We were getting on so well . . ." Ilse Nydhalm was always reluctant to end the lessons, in the first place because Karl's mathematical talent was still undeveloped, and in the second place because she disliked leaving the house.

Otto was on his mother's heels. He heard only the kindly tone in which she spoke to Karl and in the darkness fancied he saw the kindly caress. That was enough for him.

"Poor little Karl's ruining his eyesight," he said maliciously.

"How's the boy getting on, Ilse?" asked Katharine.

Ilse made a shy and quickly checked movement with her finger upraised.

"Oh, well enough, we'll soon get through it."

Otto caught this movement of hers. He liked it. He liked all the things that women did. But he felt annoyed, too, because this girl stood in some relation to fat old Richard, not that her relation to him was very clear—and with the spice of malicious curiosity that characterized him on such occasions he said darkly:

"Richard's sitting in Susanne's room. Have you ever seen Susanne's chapel? Come along and I'll let you see it."

He drew her away with him. In the kitchen through which they had to pass to get into Susanne's quarters, he fingered her frock. "That's a pretty frock you have on." He smiled winningly as he said this. Then he opened a door, showed her in, and switched on the light.

"This is the chapel," he said. And then he spun round on his heel and ran stealthily back to the sitting-room, bursting into it abruptly; nothing, however, had changed since he left it.

144

Karl was gathering up his books, and his mother was sitting at a respectable distance from him. There was nothing one could remark.

"I suppose you're going off with your friend." Katharine Hieck rose to her feet, gave Karl a light pat, said: "Good-bye, Karl," and left the room.

"Look what I have," said Otto when they were outside. He was holding out on the palm of his hand a slim iron hook with a ring at the end of it. A simple skeleton key. "Made it myself in the workshop," he announced with pride.

Karl took and examined it.

"Would you like it?" offered Otto.

Karl thought it over and then said:

"No, you can keep it, I don't need it now."

"Oh, well, if you don't need it . . ." said Otto in a small voice, ". . . oh, well . . ." and he let Karl go home alone.

In Susanne's room meanwhile Ilse was inspecting the holy pictures on the walls. She felt afraid. She was afraid of these pictures and afraid of Susanne, who looked so like Richard and yet was not like him, sitting there so silent over her knitting and watching her with penetrating eyes.

"Do you like them?" asked Richard. The pictures to him where like symbols of some mysterious algebra.

"Yes," said Ilse shyly, "very nice." She felt that this new world was one which, in spite of all his efforts to reveal himself, Richard had hitherto concealed from her, because he himself did not know how intimately he was involved in it.

Susanne nodded.

"Anybody who sits the whole day in the university can't possibly understand this."

Why did she have to snub Ilse? Once more Richard was struck by the difference between the ascetic sharpness of Susanne's face and the massive amplitude of her rump; it was the same difference that characterized his own body.

And as usual when he became aware of this discrepancy—which happened regularly in his moments of doubt or in any situation arising out of the struggle between body and spirit—it struck him that the best remedy for such incongruity would be to cut the head clean off. Whether this applied at the moment to his own head or to Susanne's he was not prepared to say. He turned away, growling:

"What ails you about the university; the university's just what it is; we haven't made it, neither Fräulein Nydhalm nor I."

Ilse was grateful for Richard's attempt to rescue her from Susanne's unknown world and to take his stand beside her. Yet she shrank within herself; what world had she to offer in place of this unknown mysterious world of holiness? What could she offer Richard? A few scraps of mathematics? Was Susanne not better equipped from the start?

Susanne laughed comfortably. She had snubbed Ilse, and was now satisfied.

"No offence meant . . . maybe I'll land in the university myself. Richard thinks I'd make quite a good scholar."

Unresentfully, although still sore at heart, Ilse replied:

"But we all of us know that there are more important things . . . things that each of us has to struggle with alone and that no amount of studying can help." And at that moment she envied Susanne with all the force of her sensitive and jealous spirit.

If only Susanne were at the university instead of Ilse, then everything would be all right, thought Richard. But Ilse in a convent?

A grotesque confusion of two spheres, a confusion of higher and lower.

Otto came in, his expression less tense than before, "The whole family together," he said, with cheerful amiability.

Ilse gave him a smile. It was pleasant to be counted in with the family. All her life she had yearned for a sister or a brother, and nothing had delighted her so much as when her father had played brother-and-sister with her; that was the game, incidentally, which had taught her to read. Richard, her big brother—a reassuring and kindly thought.

From the wall the text looked down:

THOU ART MY GOD,
I AM THY SERVANT.

Otto, seeing Ilse smile, struck an attitude; thrusting one hand into the pocket of his flapping trousers, he waved the other grandly towards the decorations. "All my arrangement," he said in an insinuating voice, waiting for a word of praise.

No doubt of it, Otto wasn't going to be put off by Susanne. For him "a creature of that kind," such as Ilse was, counted as a real woman; for him she had lost none of her femininity. The world burns inside us, not outside us, Richard could not help thinking, and it gave him a queer feeling to look at Ilse, queer to think of her womb, which he could not imagine, queer that this unimaginable womb should be capable of bearing a child. It was like blindness, queer and unimaginable, and it was a pitiful and blind tenderness that overcame him; Love as an unending task, yes, and to serve Love as a servant, as one had to serve Knowledge.

As usual there was a faint odour of incense and lavender in Susanne's room. Over the soft, high-piled bed—Susanne's bedclothes were disposed there as well as her sister's—lay a white honeycomb coverlet with long fringes that swept down almost to the floor.

Ilse said:

"Yes, it's magnificently arranged. If ever I have a house of my own, you must do it up for me, Otto."

And Richard said, half ironically, half benevolently:

"Our interior decorator."

The ultimate justification of mathematics lies beyond mathematics and yet in it; the divine end of Being lies beyond Love and yet is Love—oh, shining spouse, oh, dark death, strange confusion of spheres.

The thought of escape, of escaping to each other, had sprung up almost simultaneously in Richard and Ilse. The flickering vagueness, the invisible menace, had now brushed Ilse's heart too with the wings of panic, but the wind of its passing had brought with it the echo of a low-toned hope, a message sent from a world that belonged to her alone and not to Susanne, the hope of finding a way to be trodden by her alone and not by Susanne, the hope of a task that she alone was competent to fulfil, and not Susanne. And as her thoughts met his, Richard suddenly remembered that the Curies were a married couple and that it was possible for man and wife to help each other in scientific discoveries.

Otto had fixed up a wreath of coloured lights around the Madonna above the bed, and now he lit them up.

"That's lovely, Otto," said Ilse, peering a little short-sightedly and putting on her spectacles. Her face had now resumed its precocious look of wisdom and childlikeness, and even Richard remarked the fact.

Susanne felt a little ashamed.

"Oh, just Otto's nonsense . . . but the picture is consecrated and so there's some sense in it, too."

"The visible world is only a symbol," replied Ilse.

Could the two spheres meet in a symbol? The words were Susanne's, though the speaker was Ilse—it was not yet the Ultimate, not more as yet than a symbol and a reflection, but the universe grew silent in expectation of the Ultimate, turning within itself, setting the Word free from the infamy of the inadequate. Richard would have liked to take Ilse's hand. She was standing beside Otto, both of them slim and youthful, like brother and sister, and he wished Otto to the devil.

In the kitchen they came upon his mother.

"You're going already, Ilse?" she said casually.

Otto said in a loud aside:

"More's the pity."

But Richard was comforted by the fact that his mother had said so simply "Ilse."

On the street, it was true, he began once again with great enthusiasm to dilate on the epistemological and logical groundwork underlying every kind of research, proving once again that even mathematics and physics, in spite of their apparently unassailable precision, brought one up against these ultimate problems of the limitations of knowledge, and that these problems alone made it worth while to live a life devoted to science, indeed to live at all.

"Yes," said Ilse. She agreed with him, but in her mind's eye she saw Susanne's high-piled bed.

For behind everything stood the knowledge of the Universe, he went on, and he showed her, in terms that lacked nothing of the utmost precision, exactly how he was going to push on his own researches and how far he would advance the knowledge of the Universe. Yes, he was full of confidence—he looked down rapturously at her, as she walked beside him, small and slim, her head slightly drooping.

One single, sparsely filled tram clattered past them.

And once more Richard was convinced that in describing the greatness and loftiness of knowledge, in unfolding and communicating his life's purpose, he was also rising to the surrender demanded by love and was paying his debt in the right coinage.

As if from a remote distance, Ilse said: "I love you."

Perhaps it was a token of genuine forgiveness. Perhaps she had felt that he was tormenting himself about making the surrender. And yet it was the one thing that made his crime painfully clear to him. For this was the first time that these words "I love you" had been uttered between them, and it was she who had first uttered them.

149

I love you. Tender and terrible appeal, knocking on another's soul, bidding it open. Appeal for acceptance, tender and terrible offering up of one's own ego.

I love you. Moment of freedom between the servitude of the past and the servitude of the future.

I love you. But it was not Ilse Nydhalm who had uttered these magical words; it was the phantom of her future that had spoken, lifting her out of her own being, delivering her painfully from the setting cloud that until now had been called Ilse Nydhalm.

With the forlorn sound of these most forlorn words ringing in his ears, Richard walked on at Ilse's side. He took it as a sign of forgiveness, but the whole lawlessness of the world was again overwhelming him. And if some passer-by had offered to cut his head off his body for him, he would have welcomed the man as a friend.

4

PROFESSOR Weitprecht had come back. Richard received a postcard at the university with the request to call him: he himself could not go out yet, unfortunately; his health had not yet improved sufficiently.

Things must be bad with Weitprecht if he was not able to come to the university; that had usually drawn him irresistibly. And indeed when Richard entered his room, he was only with an effort able to rise from his seat behind the writing-table, and from the unwritten sheets of paper one could see that he had not used the idle pencil between his fingers.

"Well," he said. "You're surprised to see what a wreck I am."

Beneath his dejection one could still feel, it was true, his former urgent and apprehensive politeness, and with their old uncertain keenness his eyes still scrutinized the features of his visitor over his glasses.

"I must thank you for your reports, Doctor Hieck."

"Fräulein Magnus's work has produced very gratifying results."

"Yes, yes," said Weitprecht absently, "very gratifying results."

In the thin air of early autumn, birds were twittering in the trees along the street.

"The cataloguing of your notes is as good as finished, too, Herr Professor; I hope you'll be pleased with it."

But Weitprecht seemed to be listening to the birds' twittering. Then he said:

"Yes, I wanted to talk to you about that . . . but you see, it really doesn't matter much."

Had Weitprecht too been infected by Kapperbrunn's skepticism?

Weitprecht noticed Richard Hieck's astonishment. He ran his finger round his collar as if he felt the need of more air, although he was wearing no tie to hinder that and the neck of his shirt was not fastened. Till now Richard had never seen him except in a starched shirt and a correct little black bow-tie. Weitprecht smiled with lips that had become the thin soft lips of an old man.

"You mustn't be alarmed, Doctor Hieck . . . I shall stand up for my work with just the same conviction as before; it has merely become a little less important to me."

"But the importance of your theories stands beyond all doubt, Herr Professor."

"The objective importance certainly, my dear Doctor Hieck, at least I hope so; but their subjective importance isn't what it was. . . . Well, well . . . you see, if they hadn't sent me to Nauheim . . ." His voice became peevish. ". . . if my wife hadn't insisted on it . . . oh, well, she meant it for the best, but it was a piece of foolishness . . . yes, if it hadn't been for that, then I should probably have been the same man today." He glanced crossly and apprehensively at the door which led to the next room.

"You'll soon be quite all right again, Herr Professor. I'm sure of it," Hieck interpolated.

Weitprecht assumed a mysterious tone.

"That's just it: I don't want to in the least. . . . It's best as it has turned out . . . only the others don't know that. . . ." His bearing showed a blend of wisdom and childish ardour. But it was the same ardour with which formerly he had upheld his scientific ideas; only then it had been more disguised, and now it was more naked.

Richard waited to hear what would follow; he had understood nothing so far.

"You see, Doctor Hieck, you too have your scientific ambitions . . . yes . . ." Weitprecht came back to himself. "You've achieved very considerable things in group theory. . . . I'm right, am I not?" Weitprecht seemed to be proud of his memory; he gave a little laugh and nodded at Richard.

"That was nothing very much to speak about, Herr Professor, a sort of secondary work." Richard felt flattered nevertheless.

"Well and good . . . if it was secondary work, then you'll keep on improving as you go on and on . . . and perhaps too you'll have more luck than I've had."

Richard shook his head, and Weitprecht showed signs of displeasure.

"Luck is nothing to be ashamed of. . . . Don't you see, to hit upon the right field of work, that is a piece of luck in itself, and not to come to it either too soon or too late, that is luck too. . . . Don't you see, that is the luck of genius . . . ideas come easily enough, they're in the air . . . but to be in the right place at the right time, that is genius. . . ." His hand was pressed against his heart, and he said in a more toneless voice: "You see, I did not have that luck. . . ."

Richard hardly knew what to say.

"Many of the new advances in physics have justified the truth of your assumptions long after the event, Herr Professor."

Weitprecht ran his hand through his hair, which reared in tangled confusion round his bald crown.

"To be a forerunner is a tragic business, Doctor Hieck; I have found that out, and I hope you haven't the same fate."

But his words had found a sensitive spot in Richard, and it was now Richard who grew warm.

"But that isn't the really essential thing, whether one comes too soon or at the right time . . . the essential thing is surely knowledge."

"Yes, yes, knowledge." Weitprecht nodded his head and smiled his childishly wise and almost sly old man's smile. "Yes, knowledge . . . I've thought that too up till now . . . and there's some truth in it too. . . ." And, becoming mysterious again: ". . . That's just it . . . I have believed in knowledge, and I have committed much wrong in the name of knowledge . . ." He nodded significantly. "Yes . . ."

"Wrong in the name of knowledge? . . . That can't be done, Herr Professor."

"Oh, yes . . ." Weitprecht glanced at the door again. "And for that reason it was a good thing that they took me to Nauheim . . . and that I . . . well, how shall I put it . . . that I'm serving my sentence now."

"Oh, you're only overworked, Herr Professor."

"Are you coming to me with that nonsense, too? . . . Am I complaining? . . . I've told you that I have no wish for it to be different. . . . It's best as it has turned out. . . . It's a part of life, just as death is a part of life."

"But knowledge and wrong, Herr Professor!"

Weitprecht was tired; he merely nodded and, indicating his heart, said:

"One is punished in the place where one has sinned."

Susanne might have said that, thought Richard. Was Weitprecht going to turn nun next? In his astonishment he merely said:

"Yes, but . . . scientific knowledge . . ."

Weitprecht said quietly:

"Don't relax in your struggle for scientific knowledge. . . . It too is holy . . . but it is the holiness of life, and it makes us forget death. . . . You understand, the holiness of death. . . . Anyone who labours at scientific knowledge does his work at seventy just as he did when he was thirty . . . and finally he is struck down, struck down in the middle of it, but without reaching an end, for he has forgotten his own death. . . . An evil man with an evil heart. . . . Yes, yes, my dear friend, with an evil heart, which has committed much wrong in the name of knowledge. . . ." He stopped exhausted.

Richard could not refrain from asking:

"Do you mean religion, Herr Professor?"

Weitprecht now seemed completely broken down. But behind the mask of age and infirmity there was again a glimmer of slyness, and he gave a little fragile laugh.

"Everyone must settle that with himself. . . . Gauss was a believer, Kant was a believer. . . . Everything considered . . ." He assumed the expository tone he employed in the lecture-room. "A man who grows old without grasping the meaning of his death dies a bad man . . . without knowledge . . . no matter how much he has laboured and come to know. . . ." He started violently, for the door had opened.

Frau Professor Weitprecht came in.

"Her's talking too much, Herr Doktor," she said disapprovingly, turning to Richard.

Weitprecht became apologetic.

"I simply had to discuss with Doctor Hieck the arrangement of all my papers in the university."

"Oh, these eternal papers! . . ." she said crossly. "Have you taken your drops?"

With the old unrestraint Weitprecht barked at her:

"Yes, my papers. I know how important my work is to you. . . ."

Richard thought it was time for him to take his leave. But when the Frau Professor turned round to say good-bye, Weitprecht, who had meanwhile gone on grumbling to himself, gave him a sly and understanding wink.

155

The air glittered when he stepped out into the street. Autumn was cutting through the summer warmth with crystalline strokes. What Weitprecht had said smacked of Susanne, and yet was more comforting. Justification of the Word by the Ultimate. Oh, forlorn peal of death.

5

THE change in the weather had begun with sultry thunder-
storms, but in twenty-four hours these had been superseded
by cold steady rain, and now a premature and blindly raging
autumn was sweeping over Nature's green summer raiment.
With a clap the swimming-stations were deserted, the
woods path from the observatory was impassable by night,
so slippery had it become. Furnished with raincoat and
walking-stick, Richard had now always to take the main
road. The tram-conductors were wearing their dark winter
coats. The mill pond, after being emptied almost to the
bottom, filled itself again to the top in a few days. An icy
slanting rain swept across the football field.

Ilse walked through the urgency of this premature and
decisive autumn. When she came down the street, in her
smart raincoat fastened round the waist with a leather belt
and the collar up, she looked mature and womanly. Then
sometimes in a sudden transport they would kiss within the
doorway, and although their kisses were awkward and shy,
unworthy of a grown woman and a young man, the kisses of
fifteen-year-olds, yet all in all it meant that they had allowed
themselves to enter a sphere of incalculability.

Ilse's lessons with Karl took place now in the early
afternoons of every Monday and Thursday. This was probably due to Katharine's domestic arrangements. Otto was
seldom home at that hour; he had to return to work at two
o'clock. When he did chance to encounter Karl in spite of
this, they exchanged their usual dig in the ribs, but Otto
always rushed away and, if nobody was looking, he would

give Karl's bicycle, which stood under the stairs, such a kick in the spokes that they rang again.

On one of these Mondays, Ilse remained behind after the lesson so as to go through a new book on the theory of sets—the subject that he was initiating her into now—with Richard. As usual this took place at the table beside the window, Richard's nightly working place, and Ilse felt flattered to be sitting there. Susanne, who usually never neglected to keep her eye on them from time to time, had gone out, but that was of no great consequence, for they sat hand in hand even when Susanne came into the room, and besides they were absorbed in their work. Moreover, Katharine Hieck was in the house.

Otto suddenly tore open the door and shot into the room, as was his habit now. Ilse gave a little shriek; Richard looked up.

"You here so soon? Have you finished work already?"

"I fell ill," Otto lied.

"The morning-after-the-night-before feeling again?"

Otto muttered something incomprehensible and looked round the room as if he were searching for something. At last he asked:

"Is Karl here?"

"As far as I know he's gone long ago."

"Is Susanne out too?" Otto's voice was hoarse.

"Long ago, my son; why, what were you wanting her for?"

"Wasn't Karl upstairs?"

"Upstairs where?"

"Upstairs . . . with . . . with Mother . . ." Otto's eyes were filled with dread.

"What reason could he have to go up to Mother? . . . What are you really getting at?" said Richard with annoyance.

"Otto, there's something troubling you . . ." said Ilse.

"Yes, that he's been going the pace too much," said Richard good-humouredly.

Otto pulled out the drawers of the chest and searched in them.

"What on earth are you looking for so desperately, Otto?"

"Nothing . . . a key . . . was Karl in this room?"

"Do you fancy Karl would take it? . . . Why should he need your particular key?"

"Yes . . . that may be . . . perhaps . . ."

He sank into a chair with his face in his hands.

"Are you still feeling as ill as that, Otto?"

"No . . . let me be."

Richard became impatient.

"Otto, we have work to do here."

"You have no right to be always throwing me out . . . it's raining outside . . . I have some rights, too."

Ilse said to appease him:

"If you want the key so much you can always get it from Karl."

"I see that I'm not wanted here," said Otto and left the room.

"He's quite crazy," said Richard in an anxious voice.

No doubt about it, Otto's behaviour was annoying; in his heart Richard wished him at the devil—yes, he had done that several times already. That was connected with Ilse somehow, with Ilse's curiously womanly unwomanliness. The whole menacing incalculability of the world lowered behind it; the devil only knew what to make of it; in any case it was impenetrable. It was a good thing that the young fool was gone. And Richard repeated: "He's crazy, and he's a nuisance, too."

"Richard," said Ilse.

He kissed her absently. He kissed her hair. But there it stopped. He felt anxious about Otto.

Then as he was climbing up to the observatory in the evening, he was overwhelmed by the manifold uncertainty of Being. Most certainly what went on in one's head was calculable, that was clear and worth striving for; but what happened lower down than the head was dark and nightlike in its incalculability. To grasp the incalculable through the calculable, that was the whole task, and if that did not succeed, there remained no choice but a sharp separation of the two parts. How could one act rightly with that dividing line through the middle of one's being. Then he thought of Weitprecht's strange words about the heart, with which one sinned and in which one would be punished. He thought of the heart lying, as if it were a resultant in a parallelogram of forces, between the upper and the lower body, and although that seemed half-plausible, yet he could not conceive it with his mind. Better to separate the forces. With a quick clean stroke.

The rain had stopped. The covering of cloud was torn; moonlight fell slanting between the bright cloud fringes. A motor-car had left the grooved mark of its tires in the wet road. Richard carried his raincoat over his arm. He thought of the approaching winter, of the world withdrawn into itself, of the snowy landscape which he would have to traverse, here under the winter stars. He thought of growing old; he thought of Weiprecht and of dying. And suddenly his father came into his mind: his father had spoken of death in the same way; it had been death that he meant by his love of the night. Forlorn laughter of death. But Ilse's smile gleamed still and clear; white flowers in the night-waters.

There was not much to do at the observatory. He went across to Doctor Losska, who smiled awkwardly and nervously and smoked one cigarette after another. He was due to go for his holidays the following week and he regarded the weather as a personal insult hurled at him by the cosmos. Ten times he repeated: "And taking the average for ever so long September is far and away the most settled month."

"Natural laws are only statistical anyway," Richard replied, and he thought of the incalculability of the world, of

160

the irrefutable exactitude of intellectual processes, and of the super-concreteness of mathematics. Dread fell upon him again.

His discomfort did not leave him. He went home early. When he reached the house, his discomfort grew as it usually did and swelled into apprehension that something unforeseen had happened. But what had happened this time was that Otto was already in bed fast asleep. Such a thing had not happened for a long time.

The windows were open. The contours of the roofs opposite could be seen, beyond them the stars, hidden every now and then by flying clouds. Richard sat down on the chair beside the door and contemplated Otto, who lay there brown and slender with clenched fists, breathing regularly. Somewhere in the distance Ilse's image flitted by, but it had on the white summer coat which she had worn that night when they returned to the town from the observatory; and that time it had been raining too.

He sat on for a long time. Then he too went to bed.

He was wakened out of his first sleep by a cry from Otto. He started up and saw by the moon's light that Otto was hurriedly looking for his clothes and dressing.

"What is it, Otto? Are you ill?"

"He's been here," Otto panted.

"Who?"

"The front door banged just now."

"Why? . . . Do tell me. . . . Who banged it?"

"Who? . . . Who? . . ." Otto was already in his shoes. "Why, Karl, of course . . . who do you think? . . ."

Richard could hear Otto grinding his teeth. He was out of bed now too.

"You're crazy! . . . What do you mean by going on all day about Karl? . . ."

"I know what I know . . ." Otto was at the door now.

Richard held him back by the coat.

161

"You're dreaming, Otto! Wake up!"

But Otto tore himself free.

"I heard it . . . I heard it . . . let me go. I must catch him . . ." And he rushed away, Richard, undressed as he was, after him. In the hallway Otto slammed the door in his face. When he stepped out, all that he could hear was Otto getting out his bicycle down below and banging the front door behind him.

On his bare feet Richard heavily felt his way back through the dark lobby to the living-room. In his confusion he forgot to switch on a light. But the living-room was already lit, and his mother faced him there. He could not understand her being there so suddenly, in her dressing-gown too, and he was so astonished that all he could bring out was:

"You're dressed already?"

"What has happened?"

"Otto . . ."

"Has he come home late again? He's been at that café again, you mark my words."

"No, no . . ." Richard pointed to the door. "He's gone out."

If she had not understood before, she did now. They woke Susanne, and in their vague apprehension and the fear that through its vagueness the most brutal clarity might break at any moment, they almost quarrelled with Susanne when, still drunk with sleep, she could find nothing to say to the news of Otto's flight but: "He's possessed by the Evil One."

"Get it into your head that he's run away!" And Katharine Hieck tried to shake her awake. Still heavy with sleep, Susanne stuck her feet out over the bed and slowly stood up, glowering suspiciously at her mother, as if Katharine knew more than she divulged. But Katharine Hieck kept coming back again and again to her original idea of the café, and as something had to be done and this after all was a concrete possibility, Richard, who had meantime got his clothes on, rushed off to the Marathon Club in the café. Otto was not there; Richard rushed to the police. There they shrugged their shoulders; nothing could be done before morning. He could quite see that. He returned to the women. They passed the night in waiting.

Next morning the lock-keeper at the mill pond found Otto's body floating in the weir. His bicycle lay in the water at the bottom of the slope below the football ground. The track of the tires showed that he had ridden at full speed into the mill pond.

6

THE news arrived in the forenoon. A policeman brought it. Richard was not in; he had gone to Karl's house to see if he could not get some information there, without hope however, and simply because he could not stay in the house.

They had immediately tried artificial respiration, of course. Frau Hieck could rest assured of that; nothing they could do had been omitted. He was now—the man brought it out with real difficulty—in the mortuary. Unfortunately. So young. A tragedy.

The two women listened to the news. They tried to understand, but they could not. Katharine Hieck took the hand that was held out to her and said: "Thank you." The man asked if he could do anything, if they would like to come with him . . . it would be necessary, he was sorry to say. Katharine Hieck answered again: "Thank you," turned away, and went into the room where Otto's bed still lay as he had left it. Without a word she began to make the bed.

The man and Susanne now dumbly confronted each other. And then Susanne put her hands to her face, turned and rushed to her room, where she fell on her knees on the hassock and with tightly clasped hands and blindly raised head broke out into a hurried, stammered prayer, interrupted by ever wilder cries of: "God have mercy upon his poor soul!" Through the open door her shrill cries could be heard in the hallway, where the policeman had remained, unable to decide what he should do. He was whole-heartedly glad when Richard appeared.

Richard was breathless. He had heard the news; it was

already being spoken about. So what the policeman told him was nothing more than a sad confirmation. "I'll go with you in a minute," he said, and went in to his mother. She had made the bed and was looking round the room, and whenever she found any of Otto's things lying about, she put them neatly away in the wardrobe. From one of his trousers pockets fell a skeleton key; she lifted it up and laid it in a drawer among Otto's painting utensils.

"Mother," said Richard.

She did not interrupt her work; she went on brushing a jacket and said parenthetically, as it were in explanation: "Otto is dead."

He took her by the shoulders and said again: "Mother."

And now at last her feverishly busy numbness dissolved, dissolved in that bestial howling which overcomes a human being when death rends a piece of flesh out of him. For the sublime dignity of death springs immediately out of the animal, and the animal in all its power and majesty can be heard in the most human lament of the mother; and now that they clasped each other, it was an animal once born of her body to which she clung, and to him she was a body that had once cast him into the world and over whose head he bowed now with twisted lips to kiss it on the hair.

"I'm going to him now," he said. "Come and speak to Susanne first."

She nodded.

Susanne was still on her knees and did not cease from her supplications. And although at the moment Richard had more important things to think about, he was astonished that even death dovetailed so neatly into Susanne's world and system. Nevertheless, he seized her roughly by the arm.

"Will you please think of your mother for a change?"

She turned a tear-stained ecstatic face upon them.

"Mother, pray with me."

Perhaps it was unjust, but the behaviour of Susanne

165

seemed just on the same level to him as if he were to set about his mathematics now; the woman appeared to be in excellent professional trim; and whether it was just or unjust, or simply an effect of his tension and sleeplessness, he bellowed at her:

"You can indulge your private amusements later! Make some strong coffee for your mother, or else she'll collapse. . . . You've neither of you slept or eaten, and it will do you good, too."

He was right. Katharine Hieck was now helplessly sobbing to herself like a child. She wept for the child that she had lost, and wept too for her own life that had missed its way and was now crumbling to pieces ere real life had begun for her. And it seemed to her as though Otto had had to die, simply because he was a portion of a life that had already lost its way.

Richard went with the policeman to the station and the mortuary.

There lay Otto in the bare, somewhat grey room which smelt at once of hygiene and corruption, of white lime and a little of sewage. Three tables composed of polished marble slabs upborne on stone supports stood like altars in the centre. On one of them lay a naked brown body, the loins covered with a small cloth. Altars number two and three were empty. Against one of the walls a water-tap dripped.

Through two great windows high up in the wall the yellow sunlight fell on Otto. Yes, it was Otto; there could be no shadow of doubt about that. As he had lain in the water for only a short time, he was scarcely changed, and though the body might have a slightly puffy look, one could see all the ribs just as in the living Otto; except that they were motionless now. Otto had become a thing, immobile—yes, it was so, he no longer breathed. Not yet in the official posture of death, his head was turned a little to the side, and the whites of his half-open eyes stared obliquely upwards. The blind stare of death that they all possessed already in life; Otto had found his way home to his fathers.

This was real death, not sham death; it was real as Otto's life had been real. Could that lifeless thing there still be called Otto? But in face of this death something in Richard began to live. It was the same thing that had asserted itself the day that he had seen his father lying dead before him. Now he remembered the fear that he, still a boy, had not been able to help feeling before that lifeless body—partly no doubt because he had been taught that one must ask forgiveness of everyone who was dead for all the wrongs one had done them—and how out of that fear, intensifying and yet transcending it, the question had sprung up, whether he was in any way responsible for this inexorable and incomprehensible death, guilty through indifference or refusal to understand, guilty through persevering in his own evil isolation; and at that time the living voice in his heart had acquitted him. And now, too, when he asked himself whether he had not been a bad and regardless brother, who might have been able to prevent this calamity if he had only shown more understanding, now, too, the voice of life made itself heard, still more distinctly than in his boyhood, saying: Yes, even if you had done him wrong, wrong for the sake of the knowledge you pursue, even if because of your own obsessions you did not reach him the help which he probably asked from you, even then you would be free from any guilt. For against death no human power can accomplish anything, and you cannot die another man's death until you have come to terms with your own. This is what the inner voice of his awakening life told him; it spoke very plausibly and reasonably and yet would not have convinced him had not something greater and more remote chimed with it, something essential which in spite of its remoteness seemed nevertheless to be quite near, reminding him of the voice of

Weitprecht slowly dying towards his death, penetrated with a touch of slyness and a touch of wisdom.

But when Richard stepped over and almost as a conventional duty took his dead brother's hand to say good-bye to him, exchange forgiveness with him, and when he held that right hand in his own, then tears rose from the animal depths of his being, and he was not ashamed, but let them flow. And even if it was his animal existence that cried out in such a way, that dared cry out in such a way, soundlessly liberating him, yet the wish to keep the thinking head sundered from the animal trunk had now suddenly fallen silent, was not only not there, but had been lifted from him, freeing him, without his knowing from what burden, yet nevertheless delivering him from a nightmare:

for in the animal instinct that had cried out in him, and in the fear whose cry vibrates through all that is animal, an awareness had broken through, borne on his animal nature and yet transcending fear, a strange and unique awareness that could be found in no system and so was not demonstrable, complete in its isolation, but life nevertheless, knowledge nevertheless, and nurtured in like manner from his animal nature and his mind. And even if one should hold that this awareness concerned Otto alone, that it was merely Otto's being as it had existed and as it possibly still went on existing, and an intuition and recognition of that, it was also an awareness which, while far transcending Otto and Otto's death, embraced the totality of the world, and despite its undemonstrability and its isolation remained simple, clear, and definite, freed from all doubleness of meaning, freed from the flickering uncertainty of the burning darkness. True, the phenomenon did not last long; soon it vanished again—perhaps it had lasted no longer than a single second—but it was, like every truth, independent of time, independent of duration, indelibly there, no dream, an awareness that could never be lost of the non-spatial world of space in which every soul moves. It was knowledge—oh, one could not call it anything else than knowledge—since it arose from that enrichment of the world and that opening of one's soul to the world through which alone the world is enriched; but it was a knowledge of the most lonely kind, a knowledge which referred to nothing but itself, forlorn among the reverberations of death as death itself, from which it issued, and all-embracing like death, which is cut off from all life and yet is the goal of every single life, embracing it in its wholeness; for it is certainty itself that issues from death and not this or that logical perception, more, it is not even merely the perception of the being of this or that one among the dead, whether he be called Otto or by some other name; it is the simple and sublime knowledge of being itself, independent of any particular context of being, bound to all being, bound to every life, all-embracing in its simplicity and in the isolation of feeling, final proof of the logical, which only from this point finds its justification. And gazing at his dead brother while the tears kept rising to his eyes, Richard knew that this knowledge was love, and that love too was nothing else than knowledge.

Oh, life, thundercloud of life, rushing onward, rushing by, holy.

Knowledge too was holy; on it, too, the holiness of life was impressed. Don't relax in your struggle towards it, Weitprecht's frail voice had said. But the holiness of death was love: only death and life together formed the totality of being, and the totality of knowledge rested in death. There was nothing pathetic in that, thought Richard, and really nothing much that was religious either. Nor was Otto's lying there very pathetic; he had carried on far more pathetically in life.

Richard settled the necessary formalities and then went without more ado to Ilse. It was not only his brother's death that gave him the right to do that.

"Otto is dead," he said to Ilse, who opened the door to him in surprise.

And with the simple obviousness of great and decisive events, she paid no attention to the amazed face of her mother, who had followed her to the door, but simply said: "I must go out with Richard Hieck."

They walked along side by side. Sometimes their fingers touched. Forgiveness flowed into them from each other. He looked at her childishly serious face and the delicate furrow between her brows, and he loved this face. He tried to think of Susanne and he could not find her. The sky was rapidly clearing. When he cast an oblique glance up at the rows of houses, the windows were glittering in the sun.

V

THE lamentation of the animal broke out yet once more; that is, at the moment when Otto's coffin vanished into the ground. At that moment Katharine Hieck cried to the heavens, for it tore the last shred of youth out of her flesh. Susanne's supplications echoed over the cemetery.

An almost cloudless day arched over the opened grave. Soberly the cemetery lay in the middle of the flat land, surrounded by factories which had crept up to its walls. In the distance one could see the avenue which led to the observatory, and if one knew the place well, one could also recognize the bathing-pool as a white dot through the trees. But beyond on the hill the round dome and red walls of the observatory could clearly be distinguished, framed in the dark planes of the pinewoods, in which here and there gleamed the lighter green of some deciduous trees. Above the mountains peacefully floated a few autumnal white cloudlets. For the rest, blue, piercing blue, such as only autumn shows.

Emilie had come to the funeral. Her presence was a great help, if chiefly an external one: for when she arrived, Frau Katharine Hieck had almost fallen off her chair in astonishment, so slim had her daughter become, and the marvel of that slimming process had thenceforth formed an inexhaustible theme of conversation for Katharine and Susanne Hieck, who in this way contrived to forget much of their trouble and grief and agitation. Now the strange sister was standing beside the heavy form of Susanne in her new mourning dress, strange and slender, nevertheless a sister. And Ilse, who had no black clothes but only her dark-blue coat, stood a little distance away, she, too, straight and slender, and more sisterly than ever; it was good that Emilie had come.

As in the old days, Emilie slept in Susanne's room, deeply touched and delighted by the bridal bed which Susanne had prepared for her. And Katharine Hieck sat in childish contentment with her two grown-up daughters, delighted with Emilie's beauty, in which she saw a reflection of her own, repeating every now and then:

"What a pity that we could not send word to Rudolf!"

If Rudolf had been there, too, it would have been a real family festival. But Emilie had to promise that she would spend every Christmas at least with them.

"Let me tell you, I really couldn't stand it here for long," Emilie warned them with a glance at the sacred images.

"Oh, for a few days you'll manage," said Katharine.

Susanne sat there stolidly.

"She would soon get used to it," she said calmly.

"I have no illusions now," said Katharine.

Richard came in.

"Your little fiancée is nice," Emilie remarked approvingly.

"Fiancée?" Richard exclaimed in embarrassment. "What are you thinking of?" But the praise did him good. Susanne was at last dethroned. And her room no longer floated in infinity; it had become an ordinary part of an ordinary flat in the Kramerstrasse. And the memory of Erna Magnus seemed to have vanished, too. It was as if Otto had taken all this away and given him something else in return; it was as if a displacement, and simultaneously an illumination, of infinity had occurred.

"How can Richard think of marrying?" insisted Katharine. "He has no appointment yet."

No, he had no thought of marrying, but he saw Ilse's delicate face before him, and not with closed eyes, not emerging from the night; but clearly in a crystalline translucent landscape he saw the grey clearness of her eyes.

And in sudden opposition to his mother he asked:

"And what about the post in the observatory? In another half-year I can have it as a permanency."

Life went on. And Emilie still stayed. She got used to it, as Susanne had said.

Kapperbrunn returned from his vacation. Tanned but no leaner, rather the contrary. In his battle with his paunch he had been once more defeated.

"Back to the daily grind," he groaned.

"It isn't a grind, Doctor Kapperbrunn," said Richard. "I think that people like us are really extremely lucky."

Kapperbrunn looked up. "A shining light, aren't you? But I must say that I still feel too young for this jog-trot, day in, day out."

"I mean that we're given the chance of doing work that we enjoy . . . while other people . . ."

"My God, work that we enjoy . . . It's a job just like any other. . . . Don't you set too much store by it, or else you'll go batty just like poor old Weitprecht."

"Have you been to see him?"

"Of course . . . he's in a bad way. . . . Well, that's his reward."

"He's driven himself hard enough in his time . . . but . . ." Richard fell silent.

"And his wife—my God, what a wife! And when I think that I'll have to marry a professor's daughter like her some day or other . . . Hieck, I tell you what, it would be better to throw it all up and take to mountaineering. Have you ever climbed a mountain, climbed up the face of a real precipice?"

"No."

"Then you don't know what living is."

"Oh, yes, I know, at least I hope so," said Hieck, who could find little to say in reply to this pious scepticism.

"Don't you come glorifying knowledge to me again. . . . Knowledge is nothing, knowledge is all my eye . . . and the world laughs at knowledge, at least the present world. You're not a modern man, Hieck."

"That may be," replied Richard Hieck, "but as for knowledge, it has probably been in the same case through all the ages."

"You're a star-gazer, Hieck," said Kapperbrunn with that real grasp of the situation which was his peculiar gift, enabling him to see the surface of things rightly. "You're a star-gazer, and there have always been idiots like you. You're right there, you've found your right place."

"Yes," said Hieck, and thought of the crystalline landscape of knowledge.

"What is it your old friend Kant says again? The starry heavens above me and the moral law within me . . ." Kapperbrunn laughed. "Isn't that how it goes?"

"Yes," said Hieck, "that's right."

The moral law within me: that was connected with the heart somehow, with the heart of which Weitprecht had spoken, forlorn peal of the heart in the darkness of the night, forlorn knowledge of love, moral law, valid without proof.

"That isn't right at all," Kapperbrunn retorted, "for we're finding out now how many holes can be picked in the cosmic laws, and we'd better leave the moral laws out of it."

"There are statistically approximate values," said Hieck, but he thought: in the loneliness of the heart everything is absolute, in the heart there are no statistically approximate values, there the law is valid, and that is all there is to say.

"Oh, very well," Kapperbrunn surrendered; "and apropos moral laws, what is your summer harem doing? How are your two girls getting on?"

"They were very industrious," Richard said evasively, "and I'm glad that we were able to do Weitprecht that little service."

176

"It's a shame to lose Erna Magnus," remarked Kapper-brunn reflectively. "But you watch out, she won't stick to science long, she has too much life in her."

"No," said Richard, "she won't stick to it."

"When Weitprecht's gone," Kapperbrunn plunged on, "then there'll be another step up for everybody, and then we must see that something comes your way, too. We'll wangle it somehow. . . ." He was as ready to help as ever.

"Thank you, Doctor Kapperbrunn," said Hieck; "it's good of you to think of it."

"But, look here . . . well, don't you t'link that it's dreadful, this hierarchy, this ladder to climb, this eager waiting for a free rung to mount on? . . . It's disgusting, that's what it is . . . and then you talk about the beauty of knowledge!"

"My God! . . ." said Hieck.

Life would go on. And what with the theory of sets and group theory and all kinds of astronomical calculations one would be kept busy. And with any luck one might make an advance, a considerable advance, in the epistemological and logical groundwork of knowledge. Was that not enough?

And out of the darkness that gave one birth one would advance into new darkness, with stars glittering on the black background, stars that would glide along the surface of dark waters, shining out in the greatness and sublimity of death. Was that not enough?

And the veiled ambiguity of the past and of the future would lighten a little in the vibrations of the peal rung by loneliness, rung in the heart. Goal of the future, beyond life and yet itself life. Oh, love!

Was that not enough?

Out there life roared on its course, flowing down from afar, incomprehensible, uncanny, inexhaustible, but its course ran also through one's heart, just as incomprehensible, just as uncanny, just as inexhaustible. Just as terrible.

Was that not enough?

177

Richard went through the streets. The leaves in the garden-beds had the fading and somewhat staring freshness of autumn. The grass was shaven; narrow brown streaks ran across the smooth turf. The sky arched bright and clear. The autumn weather had settled into its proper equilibrium. Doctor Losska would have a good holiday.

THE END

Afterword

Hermann Broch

For Herman and Sylvia
"there sounds the voice."

Hermann Broch's large books, *The Sleepwalkers*, a powerful epic novel detailing the disastrous consequences of
Prussian success in the period from 1880 to the end of the
war in 1918, and *The Death of Virgil*, an extraordinary lyric
meditation on the last night in the dying of the ancient poet,
tell stories of disintegration, despair, release, and return to
the earth. These masterworks are rightly compared with
James Joyce's *Ulysses* and *Finnegans Wake*, respectively.
Whatever Broch wrote, he brought to what he was doing
such intelligence, such seriousness, preoccupations of such
breadth, and an intuitive sense of storytelling so great that
he imposes upon the reader's thoughts and his dreams like a
force of nature.

Early in his career, Broch, acutely aware of the drift in
Vienna and Austria toward social disintegration and the
conditions preparatory for war, made a conscious
life-decision to respond directly and philosophically and
morally to the events in which he was immersed. His vital
intuitions were analyzed in the metaphysical laboratory of
reason, which, in Kant's words, meant regarding "all our
knowledge as belonging to a possible system." Broch's
"possible system" was constructed mainly from what he
took from three thinkers.

Everyday actions and cultural works he measured by
Plato's triad of the beautiful, the true, and—above all—the

good. He examined them through the lenses of Kant's philosophy—through Kant's triad of *Critiques*, his *Critique of Pure Reason* and *Judgment* and his *Foundations of the Metaphysics of Morals*. And he re-tested them with the delicate spiritual instruments of Kierkegaard's intensely demanding norms for the three domains of aesthetics, ethics, and religion. Thus, Broch's essays in cultural analysis build beyond merely topical interests into interpretations that are insightful, helpful, and enduring. His essay on *"Kitsch"* is a pioneering statement about a certain kind of failed art, an art of false styles and false consciousness; "Joyce and the Present Age," with its Kierkegaardian title, shows how an artwork expresses its own time and something of the future; "The Style of the Mythical Age" describes "the style of myth" at the genesis of (European) culture and "the style of old age" at its apocalyptic end, with Kafka the present sign of a future culture; and *Hugo von Hofmannsthal and His Time*, surveying widely varying aspects of the culture of a society, a family, and an author, contains details that only a committed participant in that era would single out—and it is also—unwittingly?—autobiographical. His every essay in cultural analysis can stand many readings.

Broch demanded of himself that he always respond to requests for help, and writing often with the breadth and sometimes the intensity of a prophet, his severity burned into his life the outlines and depths of true heroism. The moral criteria he proposed for all others, he too, O rare philosopher-without-irony, had to live and satisfy. His self-imposed demands resulted in a constant wrestling with the necessary angels of art, science, and above all ethics, then in a searching for the origins and the dynamics of authentic intuitions, values, and culture. One consequence of his theorizing and experimenting and trying to engineer everything within "a possible system" was his leaving so much unfinished; but both the completed in his *oeuvre* and the unfinished are about open-ended processes. He said of *The Unknown Quantity* that he wrapped it up by means of a trick but that it remained open: "I always had the feeling of experimenting while I wrote this book, daringly experimenting (which includes the period of six weeks in which it was written), but I know that this book is not completed, that I only achieved the semblance of unity through a rhetorical trick, but that actually everything remained open." This lack of closure is the case for all his books, including *The Sleepwalkers,* finished but whose third volume is episodic and fragmented; for *The Guiltless,* which began as disparate stories that a publisher collected for a book, but which Broch, when confronted with this anachronistic assemblage, edited, composing new stories as well as an afterword to explain his changes and purposes; for the amalgam of *The Spell,* whose publication history would all by itself amount to a short essay. The central moment in *The Death of Virgil* is the gift to Augustus of the *Aeneid,* itself, of course, unfinished.

Intruding major historical crises—the Depression, Hitler, the second World War—made it extremely difficult for Broch to complete the projects he undertook. But it should be noted that all his projects were large-scale—because, obviously, each idea appeared to his thoughts by itself, separately and, in the instant, as one element among many. His system-desiring reflective mind moved from the look of a street, its architectural surface with its rare but noisy pedestrians, to a hypothetical cultural *Geist,* and even to some vast metaphysical formulation characterizing the ontology of all that which was the case in that moment. As a philosopher of experience and cognition, he insisted on the empirical presence of Being. Ernestine Schlant, Broch's most astute scholar and critic in the United States, writes that "Broch's holistic vision provided constant distractions from projects at hand. His philosophical framework was flexible enough to accomodate any contemporary problem, from race riots to modern physics, from abstract art to the Cold War. The all-inclusiveness of his vision forced a fragmentation of his time and interests and created a situation which did not allow for the completion of many projects." Perhaps many projects were left unfinished not just because he saw so much to include, but because the philosophical framework itself was never finished and his works were the content of an evolving universe, parts and wholes in an uneven development subject to constant adjustments compelled by events. *The Unknown Quantity* was projected as the first of six literary works and as many film treatments of them: only it and a related movie scenario "The Unknown-X" were actually written. Even if the forces of European history had not interfered, it would still have been difficult for him to carry out his projects, for the very acts involved in writing—planning, designing, outlining, beginning, drafting sentences—would alter the project. Broch participated in his writing and, as with Escher's etching of a hand etching the hand that etches the hand, his mind was changing as the words were inked on the paper or typed on the page. And so we can understand the lyrical meditation of *The Death of Virgil* as a large-scale symbolic act, each sentence manifesting Broch's deepest desire for existence and transcendence; the biographical and mythical events describing Virgil are inseparable from Broch's act of writing. In creating *The Virgil*, as Broch called his book, he was re-creating himself. Hence, Broch's desires for transformation, cognitive and social, are found everywhere, injecting, as he wrote of *Ulysses*, profound emotion into each and every passage, from the vital to the seemingly mechanical. Schlant has pointed out that in his writing about the physics of Einstein and Bohr and others, he stressed the idea that observations implicate the observer and he ignored other

184

features of the new physics: so too a completed text refers to the activity of writing and the writer. In this light *The Unknown Quantity* is especially interesting, for, unlike his other works, it was written quickly and reveals more intensely a moment in his development; it is a high-contrast black-and-white photograph in which Broch is seen carrying his previous book, having the look and wearing the clothes of someone scrambling for a livelihood and for shelter, and pointing with the stem of his ever-in-hand pipe to scattered piles of projects.

Broch's most positive views of art and of his own novels and poetry can be found earlier in his writing career, in what is called his first artistic phase, when he felt art must compete with science. He made Wagner's notion of the "total art work"—the *Gesamtkunstwerk*—into a quality of any artwork; he saw art as the only means to bring about a complete enough view of experience so that any work, short or long, could be held as a holographic monad of the entire society and culture of that era. But then he came to believe that the dominant expression of the modern era was not art but science, and that, when placed beside the urgent demands of the historical moment with the rise of Hitler, with the brevity of the lifetime allotted to him, with the onset of illness and an intimation of dying, the writing of a poem or a novel was a waste of time. Art had come to be a distraction from the ethical demands and religio-philosophical goals of the immediate historical situation. In the 'thirties, Broch's judgment of his life experiences and his philosophical commitments forced him to value art less than science. All artwork could not compete successfully with the logic of science in effecting a change in cognition or ethics. From the beginning he placed such heavy demands on his art that even when he saw it as his only means to earn some money, his attention strained toward other projects. Useful to the rest of us, Broch enacted these moral struggles in public; but every victory left exhaustion and a scar. His questions and methods made his searchings seem important and his pauses definitive and permanent arrivals demanding acknowledgment and response. He defined his terms and categories in such purist manner that given the strength and depth of his personal integrity, it is not surprising that his not finishing most of his projects makes it appear that he failed as a writer. His essays support this judgment in as much as they are constantly grasping for certainties. But as his works united the great poetic density with the inherent incompleteness of the life process, I wonder why he did not turn more toward a philosphy of fluid-process without a definitive end-term.

Hermann Broch was born November 1, 1886, in Vienna, to Jewish parents; his father Joseph Broch, moving from Moravia to Vienna, had made a fortune in textiles, and his mother Johanna Schnabel was the daughter of a wealthy Viennese family. Broch's family was financially very well-off, and even when a refugee, he traveled with the accoutrements of his class—hand-made shoes, each with its wooden tree, fine linens, initialed. His schooling was directed toward his taking over his father's textile company. He went to the *Staats-Realschule*, where he studied the natural sciences and French, and then the *Webschule*, the Vienna Institute for Weaving Technology. He did a period of apprenticeship in Germany, Bohemia, and England, including a two-month visit to the United States. He joined the business in 1908. His real interests, in cultural analysis, were expressed on the side by writing and seeking to publish articles and poetry and by auditing classes in philosophy and mathematics. In 1912 he sent "Notes toward a Systematic Aesthetic" to *Der Brenner*, a journal whose contributors or associates were Wittgenstein, Rilke, Trakl, Haecker, and especially Karl Kraus, whom Broch took as an intellectual model. His cultural side-line expanded to the point of entirely displacing

all his other work. He wrote about ethics and culture
following Kraus whose satiric journal *Die Fackel* sold two or
three thousand copies of each issue and whose lectures were
well-attended, in short, whose activities in the cultural and
political arenas induced in many an awareness of Austria's
daily moral and political grotesqueries. Needless to explain
how the fragmentation of the Austro-Hungarian Empire and
the rise of Hitler and National Socialism meant "dark
times," but Kraus and Broch insisting in their critiques that
they were living in the worst of times, or as Joyce said, in the
Age of Lead, was a rhetorical commonplace with poets, one
that led Kraus toward apocalypse and Broch toward historical cycles and anticipation of a new culture. Broch was the
more aware, I would say, of how extraordinary in product
and potential was this period in Viennese cultural history:
the list of his Viennese contemporaries includes Franz von
Brentano, Husserl, Freud, Klimt, Schiele, Kokoschka, Rilke,
Schnitzler, Musil, Mahler, Schönberg, Alban Berg, Webern,
Mach, Schlick, Wittgenstein, Carnap. This co-functioning of
value-disintegration and cultural brilliance became a formula describing significant cultural transitions that Broch
saw repeated in other times and places.

After serving Austria in World War I in its Red Cross,
Broch returned to responsibility for the family company; at
the same time, he continued his writing and his studies in
philosopphy and mathematics. Then, in order to devote his
time entirely to writing, in 1927, against the family's
wishes, he sold the business; and he registered for classes at
the University of Vienna with Carnap, Schlick, Menger,
Hahn, Thirring, members of the Vienna Circle, and Haas, for
courses in differential and integral calculus, philosophy of
science, relativity theory, structure of the atom, and Latin;
and from 1928 to 1930 he worked on *The Sleepwalkers*,
publishing it in 1931 and 1932. Even though the Austrian
economy was then in a very troubled state and managing the

187

business demanded too much of his time (see Broch's comments about money and inflation in 1923 in *The Guiltless*), selling the company was probably a serious mistake, coming as it did on the eve of the Depression. Broch was freed from his business responsibilities, but in a short while his family was left with little money and he with none at all, and for the two decades of life that remained to him he had to scramble to make any kind of a living. It does not seem farfetched to suggest that the mistake of selling the family business may have produced in him a trauma and guilt that are recalled in subsequent books. One senses a particular poignancy in what he writes about Hofmannsthal's father: "The secession of Lombardy in 1859 had proved ruinous for many Viennese firms, especially for those in the silk trade, and it speaks for the solid prudence of the forty-four-year-old August von Hofmann that he was able to keep the family fortune intact, apparently by way of a gradual liquidation of his interests. [. . . Just] before the boy's birth, the family fortune was devoured by the crash of 1873. No one could be held responsible for a *force majeure*, not even August von Hofmann (at that point a robust man in his late fifties), who had administered the fortune; nonetheless, feelings of guilt emerged, first with regard to the ancestry whose inheritance was squandered, second with regard to the son, who some-day would have enjoyed its benefits." Broch, who stresses the ages of Hofmann (forty-four and late fifties), the only such instances in the entire essay, was probably remember-ing that he was forty when he sold the family business. Although Broch was surely conscious of repeatedly using the Oedipal schema in his fictions, one must wonder at the number of works narrated from the viewpoint of a son with a father who is present and absolute (as in "The Romantic" of *The Sleepwalkers*) or else dead and casting his shadow over the family (as does the father-night in *The Unknown*

Quantity and the judge in *The Guiltless*). Kant's moral imperatives and Kierkegaard's ethical and religious demands pronounced awful judgments on the "unethical act" when he lost his family's inheritance to the ambitions of his art. That act may be undone, so to speak, but not with impunity, by the character Andreas in *The Guiltless* who "buys" a mother and takes on the task of supporting her for the rest of her life (in "The Bought Mother") until his suicide (in "The Commendatore"). Note the story's thesis, that "we are born into responsibility." "But it is certain that we cannot come close to God while we persist in our indifference and increase our guilt by complicity in the world's fall—a fall that is on its way to becoming unstoppable—into crime and bestiality. Original sin and original responsibility are related, and the question: Where is thy brother? is addressed to us all, even if we know nothing of the crime. We are born into responsibility, and this alone, the magical place of our birth and our being, is decisive; only our self-sacrifice as a sign of our constant revolt might acquit us." Andreas' suicide, a selfish martyrdom, is "a bullet through his temple, his legs widely parted and his arms outspread as though to be nailed to a Saint Andrew's cross." Broch's life, since he sold the business, might be seen as a constant self-sacrifice in the name of those higher ethical responsibilities conferred with "birth." These two stories in *The Guiltless* were written after the full traumatic revelation of the reports of the films of the concentration camps; also, Broch's mother, Johanna Schnabel, died in Theresienstadt. Yet his actions should not be seen as mere neurotic compulsion. He told Jean Starr Untermeyer that "it was almost a compulsion for him to accept these burdens as they came in his path. Whoever appealed for help, must be helped. This was the very cornerstone of the ethical structure to which he tried to conform." That "compulsion" is a major expression of his heroic agony. Whatever the sale did to the financial situation of his family and Broch's psychology, for the rest of his life he struggled desperately for money and for moral rectitude. He could no longer envisage any artistic activity otherwise than as, simply and definitively, a mistake, as something useless, feeble, verging on evil: his art, thereafter, was done "in spite of himself."

In 1932-34, after the appearance of *The Sleepwalkers*, Broch wrote and published several major essays, a novel, a movie scenario, a play, and more. His play "The Atonement" is at once about the bitter antagonisms of labor, management, and marketplace, and the bitter division of attitude separating men and women. The foreground conflict reveals in harsh light the men grimly destroying themselves through economic betrayals, mindless and premeditated murders, two suicides, and the semi-accidental killing of an infant. While this class battle is intensifying and its disastrous consequences are increasing, out of the shadowed fringes of background emerge the women, who are working out small but very important alternatives: one woman consoles a second woman, helps a third, and at a crucial juncture makes a kindly comment to still another. The play shows, retrospectively, that the men are waging a self-destructive class war; while the women are enduring, and forming a separate attitude, perhaps a different culture. The play ends with an epilogue of women speakers who sum up the catastrophic events of their lives in stylized language gestures, speaking not in "prose" but in verse and in solo and choric voices. I suspect that this evolution of the women characters would have continued in the novels of the series initiated by *The Unknown Quantity*; doubtless it influenced the presentation of the hysterical men and the determined women in Broch's next novel, *The Spell*, begun in 1935. Another Broch pattern is emerging: that as men bring this cultural period to a close, with a terrifying bang, women are introducing the future.

When his publisher suggested he write a novel more accessible than *The Sleepwalkers*, one that would get around and make his name better known, Broch planned a series of shorter, simpler novels that would show—not surprisingly—the integration of science, society, emotions, and cognition. Concurrent with his prolific output of the years between publication of *The Sleepwalkers* in 1932 and his departure in 1938 for England and the United States was Broch's growing preference for science. Studying mathematics upon his return to the university, participating, in the 1920's, in discussions of the ideas of Mach, Schlick, Carnap, and owning a collection of mathematics books which he sold to help finance his emigration, he was well acquainted with the radical developments in mathematics in the 19th century and in mathematical physics at the recent Solvay conferences, which involved Einstein, Bohr, Heisenberg, de Broglie, and others, who were bringing the struggles between the theory of relativity and the idea of quantum physics out of the classroom, laboratory and specialized journals and into world history. Furthermore, Broch's artistic impulse was always in the tradition of didactic art—starting with Hesiod, Empedocles, Plato, Lucretius. Wordsworth, anticipating this task of modern art and modern science, wrote in the Preface to *The Lyrical Ballads*: "Poetry is the first and last of all knowledge—it is as immortal as the heart of man. If the labours of Men of science should ever create any material revolution, direct or indirect, in our condition, and in the impressions which we habitually receive, the Poet will sleep then no more than at present, he will be ready to follow the steps of the Man of science, not only in those general indirect effects, but he will be at his side, carrying sensation into the midst of the objects of science itself. The remotest discoveries of the Chemist, the Botanist, or Mineralogist, will be as proper objects of the Poet's art as any upon which it can be employed, if the time

191

should ever come when these things shall be familiar to us, and the relations under which they are contemplated by the followers of these respective sciences shall be manifestly and palpably material to us enjoying and suffering beings. If the time should ever come when what is now called science, thus familiarised to men, shall be ready to put on, as it were, a form of flesh and blood, the Poet will lend his divine spirit to aid the transfiguration, and will welcome the Being thus produced, as a dear and genuine inmate of the household of man." Broch saw that science had already created a material revolution of great spiritual as well as material importance— and the revolution was continuing fiercely.

Broch wrote *The Unknown Quantity* in July and August of 1933, published it in serial form between September 17 and October 7, and saw it appear as a book still within the same year. He foresaw it also as one in a series of films, corresponded with the Hollywood studio of Warner Brothers, and wrote a scenario, "The Unknown-X," where the setting is on a south-sea island at a testing of Einstein's theory of relativity. Broch already had constructed a preliminary figure for Richard Hieck, the novel's central character, in his short story of 1917, "Methodically Constructed" (incorporated in *The Guiltless*), where a *Gymnasium* science teacher, Z., expresses his *ressentiment* at the vitality of the students and falls in love. (A follow-up story, written in 1947, is "Studienrat Zacharias's Four Speeches," which shows the same character resisting innovations in science, engaging in local politics, and expressing incipient anti-Semitism: the convenient catch-all object is Einstein.) Hieck resembles that earlier character through certain limitations of feeling and imagination, but rather than a teacher he is a graduate student preparing a doctoral dissertation in group-theory and a witness from within to the changes coming about in mathematical physics in 1926 and 1927. *The Unknown Quantity* is precise in its dating. Its round of a complete year with its successive seasons grounds the events in an actual and symbolic world. (Broch uses this same device of a complete natural cycle in *The Spell* with a nine-month—a feminized?—year and *The Death of Virgil* with twenty-four hours, the four classical elements, and the first week of Genesis, which, in reverse order, is the last week of the undoing of the universe.) But the chronological dating of 1926 to 1927 is a historical signal, reinforced by references to mathematical articles published in "Crelle's *Journal*," which was the *Journal für reine und angewandte Mathematik*, and allusions to events suggesting the Solvay conferences. These papers in mathematics and physics and conversations and rumors are important to Hieck's worldview, not because he is also a scientist (that only brings this news to him sooner than to the general public), but because these changes are so radical that they are going to force changes in his and everyone's sense of values, in everyone's total sense of being. Statistical analysis, quanta, uncertainty, solutions of complementarity that were set in opposition to Einstein's positions—for Broch the discussions that constituted this fundamental reconceptualization were of the extremest delicacy, with a formula emerging here, another there. It should be compared to a moment in one of Plato's Dialogues, when one proposition overcoming another went on, *mutatis mutandi*, to have an extraordinary impact on all subsequent European cultures. Another such moment is constructed in *The Death of Virgil* when, in a conversation with Augustus, Virgil delivers the unfinished *Aeneid* to the Emperor and to posterity. Those delicate shifts in the central formulas may become wide shifts in the periphery of Hieck's overall worldview and, therefore, affect every aspect of his being, from his unstated, non-rational sense of himself to his struggles with new emotions, indeed, to the way he views the path he must take when he walks to the observatory. Furthermore, even though Hieck's work in group-theory is

193

appropriate to the mathematics of the new physics, it is easy to see the relevance to Broch's novel of the work and life of George Cantor, who invented a new field of mathematics, set theory; who published two related early papers in Crelle's *Journal* (because of conflicts with an editor, Kronecker, he never again sent an article there); who believed his set theory expressed a divine cosmic meaning, whose decisions about infinitesimals appear influenced by a deep fear as much as by the logic of his mathematics; and who, later in his life, experienced profound melancholy, leading to an emotional collapse and to his hospitalization. Hieck, too, must face the eruption of, say, uncertainty in the new physics, irrationals in human relationships, and infinitesimals within the ego.

As has been pointed out, Broch's attitudes toward philosophy, science, cosmology, and ego psychology were influenced by Plato. He favored Plato's idea of rational principles, or a single principle, a *Logos*, behind or within the phenomena of the empirical world. I would like to find, contrary to the views of some very fine Broch scholars and critics— contrary even to Broch's own statements—, that he was less fascinated by the absolutes of Platonic ideas, numbers, and transcendent reality than by their function as ideal limits and provocations compelling wonderment and inquiry into the methods of arrival at absolutes. His Platonism was at times a kind of "scientific realism," by which I mean that some properties in and of nature are measurable, lend themselves to computation, and when applied produce consequences; and I do not mean, as in the silliest and most superstitious of Platonisms, that we see the numbers behind the colors of the sunset, as if a *demiourgos* painted existence by numbers. For Broch, language, like mathematics, made new things possible in the world and spirit. Yet, in a range from absolute verbal animism (where words, existence, and their mutual operations are fused inseparably) to absolute verbal alienation (where signifier and signified do not exist in the same universe and where it is impossible to use the same signifier twice, or even once), Broch's use of language is clearly closer to verbal animism. He was an animist in desiring his own transformation and the world's in and of and through the processes of cognition and writing. Just as the Platonist Mallarmé, combining grandiosity and anxiety, wrote that *"Tout, au monde, existe pour aboutir à livre"* ("Everything, in the world, exists in order to end in a book"), Hieck believed everything existed to end in his logic-founded equations, with Russell and Whitehead in his past and Gödel in his impending future. Variations of the tradition of Platonism are discernible in the artworks of Kandinsky, Schönberg, Joyce, Picasso, Duchamp, and others, but Broch's Platonism differs essentially from theirs in that underlying his are ethical demands that he applied to every aspect of life. His Platonic ethics underwrites a very conservative view of experience, urging him to reconstitute time-worn traditions, such as ennobling the identification of women with nature, and dissuading him from a more radical review that would admit new relations based, for example, on ideas of uncertainty in science and philosophy and existence.

A colleague of Hieck refers to a famous passage from Kant: " 'What is it your old friend Kant says again? The starry heavens above me and the moral law within me . . .' Kapperbrunn laughed. 'Isn't that how it goes?' " Broch wrote in a letter that *The Unknown Quantity* "should depict that condition of the soul in which the purely scientific, mathematical thinking in its extreme rationality necessarily turns into its irrational mystic opposite, approximately into that condition which Kant expressed in the phrase 'the starred skies above and the moral law within me,' and which, as absurd as it might seem at first glance, is part of the significant components of our times." And Hieck thinks:

195

"The moral law within me: that was connected with the heart somehow, with the heart of which Weitprecht [a physicist whose heart is failing] had spoken, forlorn peal of the heart in the darkness of night, forlorn knowledge of love, moral law, valid without proof."

Like the importance of Plato for this century's art and science, the importance of Kant must be borne in mind. For example, a similar nexus of the mathematics of irrational numbers, emotional agonies, and the philosophy of Kant is found in Robert Musil's *Young Törless*, published nearly thirty years earlier, in 1906. Adolescent Törless stretches on the ground and, gazing pensively into the blue sky, like Hieck into the night-sky, intuits the concept of "infinity." "He felt it must be possible, if only one had a long, long ladder, to climb up and into it. But the further he penetrated, raising himself on his gaze, the further the blue shining depth receded. And still it was as though some time it must be reached, as though by sheer gazing one must be able to stop it and hold it. The desire to do this became agonizingly intense. [. . .] Now Törless began to think about this, making an effort to be as calm and rational as he could. 'Of course there *is* no end,' he said to himself, 'it just keeps going on and on for ever, into infinity.'" Later, "during the mathematics period Törless was suddenly struck by an idea. [. . .] And now, right in the middle of the lesson, it had shot into his head with searing intensity," the concept of "imaginary numbers." His classmate explained the concept to him: " 'It's as though one were to say: someone always used to sit here, so let's put a chair ready for him today too, and even if he has died in the meantime, we shall go on behaving as if he were coming. . . .' " (I think here of Hieck's forever-present dead father.) " 'And after all, where is this so different from irrational numbers—division that is never finished, a fraction of which the value will never, never, never be finally arrived at, no matter how long you may go on calculating

away at it?' " (And here of Hieck's "valid without proof.")
" 'And what can you imagine from being told that parallel
lines intersect at infinity? It seems to me that if one were to
be over-conscientious there wouldn't be any such thing as
mathematics at all.' " But, still worrying, Törless goes to his
teacher to ask about such concepts as imaginary numbers.
His teacher's response is to send him off with a copy of Kant!
For the Törless of Musil in 1906 Vienna, the irrational
erupts as adolescent homosexuality and sado-masochism,
perhaps transitory along with adolescence: for the adult
Hieck of Broch, desirous of encounters with absolutes, the
irrational erupts in the acts of love and death. For both Musil
and Broch, the official, institutional Kant fails to counter
irrationality. Unlike Törless' teacher, Broch worked to make
Kant truly practical by re-inventing him in the present age.
In an interesting passage in his *Hofmannsthal*—a highly
judgmental passage, pointing out the guilt August von
Hofmann felt over the loss of the family fortune and the
situation of those Jews who had assimilated into Vienna's
Christian, mainly Catholic society—Broch sets forth the
principle that seems evident in the work of Kant: "For the
saying 'What you have received as your fathers' heir, earn it
to possess it!' had not only become a general bourgeois
financial axiom but, in this case, had also gained (if only
unconsciously) a meaning for assimilation, that of the
assimilation legacy which had to be upheld through the
possession of money." That is, to make money meant to
make it his own in an actual practice, and to think meant to
apply thought in art and cultural revelation, in science and
metaphysical changes, in the darkest center of the ego-body
and in ethics.

Hieck's sister, Susanne, "had been for years preparing
herself to enter a [Catholic] convent." Twenty-five years
earlier Broch had converted to Catholicism—because his
first wife's family objected to his being Jewish; because in

the decades when European *fin-de-siècle* culture and political consciousness and actions were degenerating into war the Catholicism of the Middle Ages had a special aura and attraction as if the religious institution had nurtured a coherent, creative, value-rich society; because Kraus and others converted at a time when Austria listed the largest number of conversions by Jews to Roman Catholicism of any nation in Europe; because Broch's theoretical ideal of a cultural period when values were omnipresent, requiring of the individual only judgment and will, had turned into an ideological norm, that is, he was referring to medieval times as having bred a utopian age without seeming to make any further inquiry into its historical or cultural actuality. In a late essay, "The Style of the Mythical Age," he stressed once again the unity of Christianized Europe, with the Roman Catholic Middle Ages its apogee and the Protestant Reformation a decline leading to romanticism and, finally, to secularism and the total crumbling of all values; in the modern world, every ethical problem was beheld as unique and every ethical decision was ephemeral. Yet Broch's picture of Susanne Hieck's need for Catholicism reads more like superstitious fetishism than what I think Broch was describing. Was Broch a practicing Catholic, going to confession and mass? His divorce from his first wife suggests that his was a practical and intellectual conversion, but not one of faith and dogma. Broch noted in his study of Hofmannsthal's family the question of Jewish assimilation into Christian Vienna, but he did not mention the migration to Vienna of thousands of Jews from Moravia and elsewhere in the two decades before he and his parents settled there, a migration that expanded the city's Jewish population from six thousand to seventy-two thousand, neither did he mention the development among the Jews of a variety of communal styles, religious and secular, nor, finally, the various Zionist programs including cultural Zionism. The

198

relationship of his religious criteria, derived so directly from Kierkegaard, yet seeming to remain so intellectual, and his own assimilation requires further study.

Hieck's brother Otto is a young artist who because of the family's financial needs has been apprenticed to a commercial art studio. Broch's descriptions of Otto's commitment to the visual, to the perfection of artworks, his descriptions of Otto's unsatisfying repetitive behavior and of his skills at decorating his sister's bedroom-altar show him to be a version of Kierkegaard's (futilely repeating) aesthete, increasingly obsessed with his widowed mother's renewed sexuality. Broch had been interested earlier in Otto Weininger's *Sex and Character*, but in his novels and stories he uses a reductive version of Freud's Oedipal analysis. The presentation of the mother is not much developed in *The Unknown Quantity*, and she appears similar to women in *The Sleepwalkers* and "The Atonement" and, standing with her mathematician son, she anticipates in faint outline Mother Gisson and the doctor in *The Spell*. A brother Rudolf is away, and a sister, Emilie, who was away, returns at the end, each seeming to act out desires beyond Richard's comprehension.

The four main characters form a distinctive schematic order suggesting that Broch used a modern version of medieval humours or the four psychological functions of sensation, feeling, intuition, and thinking posited in the psychology of C. G. Jung, whom he met about this time. But their individual dynamics seem derived from Kierkegaard's triad of the aesthetic, ethical, and religious. Shortly after *The Unknown Quantity* Broch used astrological and geometrical signs, as "primordial symbols of the soul," or intentional structures, in the stories written in the 'thirties and incorporated later in *The Guiltless*: these he called "Zodiac Stories." Of course, appropriate to a novel where mathematics, physics, astronomy, the theory of relativity, moral laws and cosmology are woven into the story would be a family that formed and functioned together like the stars of a human constellation. Broch's combining in a novel the categories and dialectics of physics, the formulism of mathematics, and Jungian typology may have been the reason he declared that "I always had the feeling of experimenting while I wrote this book, daringly experimenting." His experiment was like that of the scientific plays of Ben Jonson.

These years, which may be seen as Broch's middle artistic period, were more and more dominated by the destructive violence of Hitler and the National Socialists. In 1935 Broch began *The Spell*, which he described as about Hitler and his followers; however, it is a mistake, made by some critics, to accept this as a simple identification: the story of the battle of Mother Gisson and Marius Ratti had been anticipated in the women and men of "The Atonement," which had nothing to do with Hitler. *The Spell* is more about the transformation of a community, about mass hysteria or what Wilhelm Reich called "emotional plague." Later, when Broch devoted greater attention to mass psychology, it was still in relation to Hitler. His proposal for a grant to study mass hysteria begins, "A psychopathic has made this Time what it is. Manifold are the causes for both [his] rise and the world's inertia in letting him do as he pleased. While the German nation has elevated that man Hitler, followers and admirers of his are still to be found all over the world. Even his very downfall will not do away with Hitlerism as such. [. . .] Has mankind entered then a psychopathic stage? Are the many horrifying traits displayed by the present human masses to be dealt with psychopathologically? [. . .] In order to clarify the problem, the author has to approach the psychical behavior of the human masses." Hitler scraped fiercely at his nerves.

Early in the 'thirties, Broch had been invited by Willa and

Edwin Muir, his translators, to go to England. Exactly on the day of the *Anschluss*, March 13, 1938, he was arrested, but through the efforts of writers, such as Franz Werfel, after just a little over two weeks in prison he was released, on March 31. Immediately, he began his emigration from Austria to England and Scotland, then to the United States. In the United States he continued the same struggle to make ends meet that he had waged in Austria, now no longer threatened by Hitler but with the problems a refugee faces. He received help from other German-Austrian emigrés, and he worked at an office in New York City run, I believe, by Hannah Arendt, for helping Jewish refugees; he lived in Erich Kahler's house in Princeton from 1942 to 1947. However, in his dozen years in the United States, he never ceased to be a supplicant at the gates, and letters, applications, proposals show him trying to find an economic foothold. That scramble had been his financial fate for twenty years.

In 1937 he received an invitation from the Austrian radio network to speak about Virgil. The occasion was Virgil's birthday; but surely it was not the calendar forcing recall of Virgil at this time as much as the desire to hold back the destruction of European culture, just as after World War II Goethe's birthday was celebrated so as to signal the cultural restoration or reconstruction of Europe. Broch recognized such purpose and made his work on Virgil the occasion for reflecting upon the two thousand years of the European Christian era from the historical Virgil to the present, and backward, so to speak, another two thousand years from Virgil to the cosmogony of Genesis. Virgil was the monadic point between. In keeping with his desire to see everything systematically, Broch had theories of history and culture that had peaks of unity and valleys of disorder: cycles of two millenia formed a long-term sine-wave. Broch had many antecedents in this, from Hesiod, Empedocles, and Plato through Joachim de Floris to Vico, Hegel, and, most recently,

Spengler. The style of *The Virgil* fulfilled more even than *The Sleepwalkers* his view that new knowledge required new forms. In *The Virgil* he re-composed thoroughly Novalis's *Hymn to Night* as a lyric oceanic meditation in massive sentences. Aldous Huxley who saw a selection advised Broch in a letter to make shorter sentences. "Broch dictated to me," writes Jean Starr Untermeyer, "his reply to this letter, telling Huxley that it was when he was in a Nazi prison, with the possibility of his own death not far off, that the germinal ideas of the work in question first came to him, and in just this form: long, wavelike sentences, mounting slowly to a peak and receding, their crescendos and diminuendos following each other like the oceanic surge of an incoming tide. He must, he wrote, be true to his experience [. . .]." This result evolved into the difficult, extraordinary, deeply moving *Death of Virgil*, which was published in English before it was in German in a translation by Jean Starr Untermeyer, who herself is an unfairly neglected poet. A beginning of this meditation in a different style began, it may be suggested, in the six-week writing of *The Unknown Quantity* in which Hieck meditates in nightthoughts about cosmic and emotional order and disorder. After completing *The Virgil* he completed *The Guiltless* and began work again on *The Spell*, and he continued his studies in mass psychology, his true interest at the time.

Broch's first marriage in 1909 to Franziska de Rothermann ended in divorce in 1922. The son from that marriage, Hermann Friedrich Broch de Rothermann (born in 1910), translated and published Broch's play "The Atonement" and *The Spell*. In the winter of 1950-1951 Broch married a second time. His new wife was Anne-Marie Meier-Graefe, widow of the art-historian Julius Meier-Graefe; she was, so she said (in conversation, March 23, 1959), the model for Plotia in *The Death of Virgil*.

In 1947 Broch suffered a compound fracture of his left

arm, and in 1948 severely fractured his left hip, spending almost a year in the hospital at Princeton. When he was released he was unable to navigate the stairs in Kahler's house and moved to New Haven where three years later, on May 30, 1951, he died at the age of sixty-four of a heart attack.

In view of the range and quality of Broch's fiction and non-fiction it is important that everything he wrote be accessible in English, that his out-of-print works be reprinted and the vast remainder translated and published. The Muirs, most famous for their Kafka translations, translated *The Sleepwalkers* immediately after its appearance in German. *The Unknown Quantity* was brought out in German in late 1933 and it too was immediately translated by the Muirs, to be published in English in 1935. *The Death of Virgil* appeared in Jean Starr Untermeyer's English translation before it appeared in German. No such speed has been shown, unfortunately, for the many volumes of Broch's studies in mass psychology, his theory of democracy, his essays, and his poetry. Those of Broch's books available in English at this date include *The Sleepwalkers*, *The Spell*, *The Death of Virgil*, *The Guiltless*, and *Hugo von Hofmannsthal*, all in excellent translations. Ernestine Schlant's indispensable *Hermann Broch*, a biography with commentary on the works, reprinted in 1986, was the source of most of the biographical information here and a few quotations; her essay "Hermann Broch and Modern Physics" is particularly germane to *The Unknown Quantity*. The description Jean Starr Untermeyer gives of Broch in her memoir *Private Collection* is "*ruhrend*," as Broch said of her, touching, very touching. I have found Broch's intellectual and ethical and artistic life heroic and touching. Whatever his philosophical idealism, his combination of Plato, Kant, and Kierkegaard, his conservatism, his tendency to write in abstractions (which he must have felt as palpably as composers do their notation or mathematicians their equations), I find him always returning to the human earth. As it appears to Richard Hieck, sitting next to his sister,

"All streams of life flow into the quietness of night, all streams of remembering and forgetting. Cast upon the earth, man breathes, and his dream rises from the earth into the sky. Does space breathe? Does it expand to the millionth power, does it contract to that infinitesimal point in which space ceases to have any extension and is changed into the vibration of a forlorn note? [. . .] To come back to earth night after night, to hear its vibrant note, the note that swells to fill the whole universe, to an intuition of the whole universe, and yet leaves nothing behind but a small act of knowledge: that was all one could desire. A million light-years, a thousand light-years, that was a number like any other. With shy, awkward fingers he touched her shoulder. "Go to sleep now. You're tired. Good night.""

—SIDNEY FESHBACH
City College: CUNY
1988

This book was set in Trump Medieval by
American-Stratford Graphic Services, Inc.,
of Brattleboro, Vermont,
and printed and bound by
McNaughton & Gunn, Inc.,
of Ann Arbor, Michigan.

TMP